THE GATEWAY

GLENN G. THATER

This book is a work of fiction. Names, characters, places, and incidents either are the product of the author's imagination or are used fictitiously. Any resemblance to actual persons, living or dead, events, or locales is entirely coincidental.

THE GATEWAY
Copyright © 2009 by Glenn G. Thater.
All rights reserved.

Published in the United States by CreateSpace, A DBA of On-Demand Publishing LLC, part of the Amazon group of companies.

ISBN-10: 1-4495-6915-3
EAN-13: 978-1-4495-6915-0

Visit Glenn Thater's official website at:
http://www.angletheta.blogspot.com

Manufactured in the United States of America

First Paperback Edition: October 2009

10 9 8 7 6 5 4 3 2 1

BOOKS BY GLENN G. THATER

THE HARBINGER OF DOOM SAGA
THE GATEWAY
THE FALLEN ANGLE
KNIGHT ETERNAL

HARBINGER OF DOOM
(Combines *The Gateway* and *The Fallen Angle* into a single volume)

OTHER WORKS

THE HERO AND THE FIEND – appears in the Anthology *Shameless Shorts*

CONTENTS

Preface		v
I	Valkyries Gather	2
II	The Wailing	4
III	On Magic and Mummery	18
IV	The Prayer	20
V	Dargus Dal	23
VI	Dor Eotrus	25
VII	The Circle of Desolation	28
VIII	Chaos, Coins, and Cults	31
IX	Mister Know-it-All	37
X	The Fog	52
XI	The Temple of Chaos	57
XII	The Hero's Path	72
XIII	Your Time has Come and Gone	81
XIV	Lord of the Land	85
XV	Epilogue	95
Glossary		96

PREFACE

The Gateway is the first story in a collection of the adventures of the ancient warrior-hero most commonly referred to as Angle Theta.

Although the original historical manuscripts detailing the life and times of this classic warrior are still inaccessible to the general public, my contacts and travels have afforded me rare opportunities to view and even duplicate some of the original manuscripts which consist of more than ten thousand documents stored in protected archives in twelve museums and universities scattered across seven countries.

Due to the inaccessibility of these documents, few modern scholars or authors are familiar with the "Thetian manuscripts." Consequently, the general public knows little or nothing about this ancient hero who some scholars believe helped shape much of the ancient world and perhaps was the historical inspiration for the legends of Beowulf, Gilgamesh, King Arthur and others.

Until now, no scholar has attempted a detailed compilation of the entire Angle Theta saga, although several notable works containing Thetian stories have been penned through the centuries. Grenville's work "Ancient Warriors of Scandinavia" (1884) and Addleson's "The Ancient Cities of Prehistoric Europe" (1921) both contain several stories of Theta's exploits. The text "The Warlords" (1408) by Chuan Chien contains two tales of Theta's adventures in ancient Asia. While there is no complete English translation of Chien's text, the accounts contained therein serve as independent evidence of the existence of Theta as a historical figure. The essay "Forgotten Empires" by Charles Sawyer (1754) and Da Vinci's manuscript "Of Prehistory" (1502) also contain story fragments and references to the historical Theta. The voluminous treatise "Prehistoric Cities of Europe" by Cantor (1928) presents noteworthy, though non-conclusive evidence of the historical existence of the city of Lomion in what is now southwestern England.

Some modern scholars do not accept the historical efficacy of the Thetian manuscripts due to the relatively small quantity of corroborating archeological evidence for the ancient cities and cultures detailed therein. Thus, they relegate Theta to the realms of myth, legend, and allegory. Others maintain that the scholarly texts mentioned above, coupled with the original archived manuscripts, serve as sufficient evidence to verify the historical existence of Theta, the man. One can only hope that in time the archeological record will further reinforce this position.

Several years ago while researching Theta for a story that I had planned to write, I had the good fortune to meet and begin a long-standing collaboration with several leading Thetian scholars, most notably Professor Augustine DiPipcorno of the University of Padua, and Dr. Ann Lewis of The University of Indiana, who have for some years been actively translating the entire body of available original manuscripts. These professors are leading a team that is currently preparing a series of detailed scholarly texts that include all the original tales plus their commentary and thorough critique of the corroborating scholarly, historical, literary, and archeological evidence.

The work you are now reading, however, represents my re-envisioning of the first volume of the Professors' translations into modern prose with additional dialogue and descriptive language added so that these stories will be found more accessible and entertaining to the typical reader. Further, I have sometimes chosen to label certain fanciful creatures and devices described in the original manuscripts using names and words that are familiar to modern readers of fantasy and science fiction tales. The story and chapter titles are my own and are meant to be entertaining. In all cases, however, the central plots, facts, themes, and spirit of the original tales remain unchanged.

I hope you will come to enjoy the Thetian tales as much as I have. Please feel free to leave any constructive comments in the comments section of my official website at http://www.angletheta.blogspot.com and/or in this work's listing on Amazon.com. Happy reading.

Glenn G. Thater
October 25, 2009
New York

THE GATEWAY
An Excerpt from The Saga of Angle Theta

"You will not thwart us again, harbinger of doom!
We shall have this world this time.
What once was ours will be ours again!"
- The Chaos Lord Bhaal to The Lord Angle Theta

I
VALKYRIES GATHER

A grayed Lord and his lieutenants stood at the fore of a small wedge of armored soldiers, veterans all. Malignant, clinging mist wafted about, sickening the men and clouding their vision. With the mist came a thunderous cacophony that consumed the night, piercing the very souls of those unfortunates within its demesne. A maleficent, skirling, bestial sound, akin to naught in nature and much in nightmare. A preternatural wailing it was, and in its wake bounded death.

"All hell's fallen on them," said Lord Eotrus.

Par Talbon made to move forward, but the old knight's hand darted out and held him fast.

"We hold our ground," said Lord Eotrus, gripping the small man's shoulder tightly. "We cannot advance in this mist and you can't turn it all. Stern's fate is in Odin's hands now." Staring into the mist he drew forth his sword from its ornate scabbard and raised the steel blade to his face - a salute from olden times - then lowered it again, though he kept it at the ready. "As is ours," he said. "Our path is clear."

"What's out there Aradon?" said Brother Donnelin. "What are we facing?"

"Nothing of Midgaard, my good priest," said Lord Eotrus. "Nothing of this world."

The wailing grew ever louder. A deep rumbling sound began and quickly intensified. Soon, the very earth itself began to shake and shudder. Archers closed ranks before their lord and his lieutenants. Swordsman and pikemen stood at the ready, eyes wide but feet planted. Several cloaked men with staffs matching his flanked Talbon.

Lord Eotrus's gaze drifted upward to the midnight sky. "The Valkyries gather. Soon they'll carry us home." More quietly then, "I thought I'd have more time. Thank Odin at least the boys aren't here."

Donnelin and Talbon exchanged worried glances as they stood protectively about their lord.

"Here they come!"

"I still can't see them," said Donnelin. "Damned mist."

"Keep your formation men!" said Lord Eotrus. "Talbon! Dispel the mist! Now!"

At his liege's command, the sorcerer uttered forgotten words of eldritch power; secret words lost to all but the chosen few. The ancient sorcery he called up crushed the unnatural mist back against the night, though the darkness lingered beyond the limits of the soldiers' torchlight.

Lord Eotrus's face grew ashen and his eyes wide as the horror thundering down upon them came into view. A war cry burst from his throat and he charged forward to meet his fate. A few of the bravest soldiers followed him, but most dropped their weapons or froze in a panic. Not one even bothered to try to flee.

II
THE WAILING

Angry wood screamed as the stairwell door burst open. Brother Claradon Eotrus's hand went to his sword hilt as several figures flew through the portal onto the tower's roof. Par Tanch spun toward them, death flaring in his eyes and blue fire licking the apex of his staff. But the wizard lowered his ensorcelled weapon, and his aspect softened at the sight of Sir Ector Eotrus's haggard face. At the young nobleman's heels were his diminutive comrade Ob and a glinty-armored leviathan known as the Lord Angle Theta. Behind them came one Dolan Silk, a wiry man of sickly pallor and strange ears.

Ector approached his older brother and Tanch, Ob following, whilst Lord Theta strode past them to the crenellated parapet. Enshrouded in a midnight cloak, Theta stood transfixed, gazing westward through the starlight at the Vermion Forest. Dolan Silk melded into shadow.

"Master Ector, thank the gods you've returned safely," said Tanch, though his gaze was affixed on the mammoth figure at the parapet.

"What's happened here?" said Ob.

"We heard a patrol disappeared," said Ector.

Tanch ignored them, still staring at Lord Theta.

"We're talking to you man!" shouted Ob. "Tanch!"

Tanch turned back toward them; an inscrutable expression on his face.

"Where's father?" said Ector. "Where are Sir Gabriel, Brother Donnelin and the others?"

"Oh it's dreadful Master Ector, just dreadful. Your father's gone missing."

"They're all missing!" said Claradon. "Father, Brother Donnelin, Par Talbon, and all the rangers. They never returned from the Vermion."

Ector's face blanched. His mouth agape, too stunned to speak.

"Stop shouting you fools," said Theta, his eyes never straying from the distant wood, his hand gesturing to quiet the others.

"And Sir Gabriel is in the mountains somewhere," said Claradon, more quietly this time, as he glanced back toward Theta.

"A hunting trip," said Tanch. "Can you believe that? The world's ending and he goes off hunting."

"Ector, who in Odin's name is that?" said Tanch, gesturing toward Theta. "And where did the other go?" he said, looking about for Dolan.

"We've got to find out what happened," said Claradon. "We've been debating all day and we're not getting anywhere."

"I'll certainly not stand here whilst my father lies dead or dying or worse," said Ector. "We must fly."

"Zounds!" said Ob, "I'm with Ector on this, what're we waiting for; let's get moving." Ob turned back toward the stairwell, then froze. He cocked his head to the side and his prodigious ears twitched up and down in strange fashion, as the pointy ears of gnomes are sometimes wont to do. "What the heck is that? That don't sound right natural to me." Ob held up his hand to silence the others. "Can you hear it?"

"Hear what?" said Ector.

"Oh no, not again," said Tanch. "Please don't let it start again."

"The wailing," said Claradon.

"Gods preserve us," said Tanch.

Frantic servants scrambled hither and fro covering the war room's windows with thick draperies, pillows, and great tapestries to drown out the unnatural din that demanded entry. Claradon paced back and forth near the head of the ponderous oaken table that dominated the room; a vacant expression covered his face and sweat beaded on his brow. Ob berated the servants for their slowness then climbed up on the chair that Brother Donnelin had made for him and plopped down into the seat, his chainmail armor clanking against the hardwood. The finely crafted mahogany chair was so tall that when the old gnome sat in it, his head was nearly level with those of the others. A servant passed him a bowl of softened wax from which he plucked a finger full to stop up his ears. "Ah, now that's much better," said Ob. "Now I can think straight again. Claradon, I'll be wanting your tale of what you know of your father, and of this foul wailing, and I'll be needing it quick. So gob up your ears with a slab of this stuff so your head'll be on straight, then start your telling."

Claradon made use of the wax then continued his pacing, ignoring Ob.

THE GATEWAY

Dolan Silk found a seat, promptly leaned back, and put his boots up on the table's edge, seemingly oblivious to the skirling sounds that still found their way inside. Ector and Tanch sat to Dolan's right, and each made use of the wax in turn. Before taking the seat across from Dolan, Lord Theta propped his massive battle shield against the wall. The old shield was sorely battered from untold battles, yet so highly burnished was its surface, much to Dolan's credit, that one could clearly see their reflection within its depths.

A disheveled servant crashed into the room. "Master Claradon, Sir Gabriel has returned. He's on his way up."

Claradon sighed in relief and found a seat near the table's head.

"Thank goodness!" said Tanch. "Sir Gabriel will know what to do. He'll clear up this troubling business."

Soon they heard Gabriel shouting from down the hallway.

"I can't leave you people alone for even a few days without all hell breaking loose. My first darn hunting trip all season. Where are Aradon and the boys? What the heck's going on? What's this damnable din? Someone answer me, for Odin's sake!"

Guards and servants scattered before his wrath. One servant tripped and landed on his face as he passed the war room's door. The flustered retainer barely managed to scramble out of the way as Gabriel stormed into the room, his left hand gripping his sword hilt. As he entered, he rapidly scanned each face, as if searching for someone. His eyes widened as he spied Lord Theta, but his gaze lingered for only a moment before he turned his attention to the others.

"What's going on here?" said Gabriel, "What's this noise and who's gone missing? Someone speak up," he said, his withering gaze clearly focused on Claradon.

"Father is missing. So are Brother Donnelin and Par Talbon and all the Rangers. It's a long story. I sent out the scouts at first light. No word yet. The garrison is gearing up, and I've tripled the guard in the Outer Dor."

"By Odin," said Gabriel. "This is what I get for taking a holiday." But his aspect softened as he moved to Claradon's side. "You've done well." They clasped arms in a firm embrace. "Aradon is in good hands - Par Talbon is most capable and Stern and his men are amongst the best woodsman north of Doriath."

"Pardon my interruption good Sirs," said Tanch, "but protocol requires that I introduce a visiting dignitary."

At this, Theta adjusted the meticulously groomed moustache that dominated his rugged features, rose, and strode confidently toward the new arrival. Theta's ornate plate armor was enameled deep blue and damasked with a proud and noble standard upon its breastplate. His long stylish cloak, although open at the front, partially obscured the two exotic curved swords sheathed at his waist. Dolan scrambled to his feet and followed his master.

"Sir Gabriel Garn, this is the Lord Angle Theta, a renowned knight errant from a far-off land across the sea. Attending him is his manservant, Dolan Silk."

"When I heard your name," said Theta, "I thought you might be the Gabriel I knew of old. Now I see that I was correct, though I've feared you dead these many years."

"Death has not caught me yet, my Lord, though it pursues me relentlessly. It's good to see you again," he said.

"Friend of old times," said Gabriel as they firmly clasped hands.

"Friend of old times," responded Theta. "It's good to see you too."

"How is it you know this here fellow, Gabe?" said Ob. "We just met up with him on the road the other day and he tells of how he never set foot in Lomion afore this week. Besides, in all the years I've traveled with you, I've never laid eyes upon him, nor heard tell of his name."

Gabriel frowned and paused a moment, locking his gaze on Ob before responding, "We served together many years ago, my friend. But those are stories for another time. Now, who can tell me the details of what has happened here?"

"The timing of your arrival is most fortuitous," said Tanch, "as Master Claradon and I were about to relate the tale to Lord Theta, Ob, and young Master Ector, who only just arrived themselves. If you gentlemen would be so kind as to take your seats," said Tanch in his most deferential tone, "perhaps Brother Claradon will begin the tale."

"Start talking, boy," said Ob. "Where are your father and the others?"

"Claradon," said Gabriel as a servant passed him the wax bowl, "Start at the beginning and leave nothing out. Good thinking about the wax."

"The wizard's idea, of course," said Ob. "Nobody better at avoiding pain or work."

"Harrumph," went Tanch.

Claradon somberly related the mysterious events of the past few days. He told of how five nights previous, horrible, guttural sounds began to emanate from the Vermion Forest to the west of Dor Eotrus, the magnificent fortress in whose central tower they were now gathered. The patrician diction in which he spoke marked him as having studied under some of Lomion's finest scholars. Similarly schooled, his brother Ector's coloring and slightly ill-favored features branded him as one of Lord Aradon Eotrus's sons. Happily, Claradon was said to somewhat resemble his mother.

"The sounds began around midnight and continued unabated until dawn," said Claradon. "Later that morning, father sent a patrol of soldiers to investigate. They discovered a strange area within the wood, completely desolate and devoid of life. The place was flat, perfectly circular in shape, and some fifty yards in diameter. They say the ground within consisted only of hardened gray soil and dust; featureless, save for some scattered stones. They found no invading army, and no strange animal or troll spoor; no clues whatsoever as to the origins of the sounds or the circle. The men withdrew and returned without incident to the Dor. Later we learned that residents of the outlying farms had heard similar sounds the night before we first heard them at the Dor."

"Where in the Vermion did they find this circle?" said Gabriel.

"Two hours ride through the wood, nearly due west."

"Then it's near the old stone ruins."

"That's what I thought as well, but the men say they didn't come across them. The following night, the strange sounds resumed. As before, they commenced around midnight and continued unabated until dawn."

"That wretched wailing kept the whole Dor up all night," said Tanch. "Without the wax it was unbearable. My poor ears were --"

"That night, however," continued Claradon, "from atop the Dor's towers the moonlight revealed a dense fogbank centering on the desolate zone. The next morning, father sent out a second patrol to investigate the strange phenomena.

"When they got back, late in the day, they reported that the diameter of the desolate area had expanded to over one hundred yards. Again, nothing else was found.

"Father decided the area should be investigated during the evening hours. He felt whomever or whatever was causing these strange goings on was hiding amidst the fog.

"The next patrol left at dusk and was led by father himself." Looking toward Theta he continued, "He was joined by House Eotrus's high cleric, Brother Donnelin; Par Talbon, our House Wizard, and his apprentices; our three rangers; eight knights, and a half squad of archers. Before he left, father ordered that in the event - in the event that he did not return - I was to await the return of Sir Gabriel or Ob before taking further action. Father had sent scouts to locate you," gesturing toward Gabriel and Ob, "shortly after the circle was first discovered, so we hoped you'd soon return."

"Get to the point, boy," said Ob, "What became of the patrol?"

"I'm getting there; have patience. Very late in the evening, shortly before midnight, the guards atop the battlements spotted the fog. It appeared to have expanded still further from its extent the previous evening. Shortly thereafter, the horrible sounds began anew. This time, though, they were even louder. Then began a series of bright flashes of light and at least two thunderous explosions that shook the keep. Par Tanch and I were atop the central tower, watching."

"What make you of them flashes and explosions, Tanch?" said Ob. "Was it a storm over the wood, or something else?"

Tanch hesitated, and looked over at Theta and Dolan. "I'm not sure that—"

"Do you think the arcane arts were invoked?" asked Gabriel.

"I -- well, I wouldn't --"

"It's all right, such things are known to our guests; you should speak freely."

"Very well then. Yes. I have no doubt that they were magical discharges and that the fog itself is of a sorcerous nature. Lord Eotrus's party clearly engaged some enemy force within the fogbank and powerful spells were thrown by one side or both. My apologies, Lord Theta, but I didn't think it appropriate to mention things arcane. Besides, this is all so hard to imagine. A Lord of a noble house attacked on his own lands by sorcery. It's unfathomable. The nerve, the audacity, the--"

"The sounds," said Claradon, "continued until first light. Father's patrol failed to return; their fate unknown. A full day and this much of the night has passed since their disappearance, and the fog and maleficent sounds have continued in the same pattern. We all saw the fog from the high tower only minutes ago. Tonight marks the fifth night since the sounds were first heard."

"What are we to do?" said Tanch. "Oh my, we--"

"We have other problems as well," said Claradon. "Rumors are spreading through the Dor. They say - they say that father is dead. They say they're all dead and that whatever's in the damnable fog will soon attack and kill us too. The people are beginning to panic."

"Bah," spouted Ob as he rose and pounded his small fist on the table. "Who cares what them folks say; they don't know nothing from nothing. Your father's alive," he said, his voice wavering and his face contorting as he tried to stay his emotions, "till I say he's not. Do you hear me, boy? We'll be going to them woods and we'll be bringing him back, I say." Quaking, he sat back down, and loudly blew his bulbous nose into his handkerchief.

"Those ruins," said Tanch, "There's nothing there but a few scattered pillars of some peculiar black stone, and one crumbling building. Looks like some sort of old temple perhaps. Sir Gabriel, you remember, we rode out there once together. You must've spent half the day staring at those ruins. That wretched place made my very skin crawl. And it wasn't just me, the horses felt it too. We had a difficult time keeping them calm near that fell place. As I recall, there was no game to be found within a mile or more. That's why we never hunt out that way, you know. The whole time we were there, I felt like we were being watched by someone or something that wasn't there – as if the place was haunted."

"Bah," said Ob. "Don't start spouting fairy stories Tanch. Ain't no such thing as hauntings."

"I'm not saying it was haunted. I'm just saying that's what it felt like when I was there."

"So who's been doing all the wailing, and yelling and such each night?" said Dolan.

No one responded; no one seemed to have an answer.

Lord Theta leaned forward and spoke in a strong measured voice. "Speak more of these ruins, Gabriel."

All eyes turned to the foreigner and then to Gabriel.

"Par Tanch is correct," said Gabriel. "Tis a dark and evil place. As for the ruins themselves, they're old, very old. Ancient." He stared across the table at Theta for several seconds, seemingly considering whether to continue. "I believe that they were not human made."

"I'm doubting that Gabe," said Ob. "Dwarves and gnomes wouldn't build in a wood. Elves and hobbits don't work much in stone, and lugron and their kin don't have the brains. Humans had to make it; there's nobody else it could've been. But who cares about the darn ruins anyways? All I care about is what happened to our people.

"They must've been ambushed. That's the only way that patrol could've been defeated or captured to a man."

Tanch shook his head. "Between Par Talbon, Brother Donnelin, and Talbon's apprentices, we had a formidable magical force in the field that night. Such men cannot easily be overcome."

"And rangers cannot easily be taken unawares," said Gabriel. "There's more to this than a simple ambush."

"Is it possible that those flashes and explosions were spells thrown by the enemy, against our patrol?" said Claradon.

"Aye, maybe that could be Claradon," said Ob, "Some type of magical ambush. But Aradon is no fool; I doubt he or Stern would walk into such a thing."

"Perhaps they met some enemy force so powerful it overwhelmed them quickly," said Tanch.

"Perhaps this, perhaps that. We'll not know nothing until we get our behinds out there," said Ob. He looked over at Gabriel. "Only question is - who and how many is to go?"

Gabriel paused for a few moments, gathering his thoughts. He turned toward the younger Eotrus. "Ector," he said, "you are needed here."

Ector grumbled and clenched his jaw, but offered no protestations.

"You must take command of the Dor, and try to quell the panic of the people." Shifting his gaze he said, "Claradon, in your father's absence, you are Lord of the Dor. The expedition is yours to command."

"--Unless he defers command to the Dor's Castellan," said Ob, "Which he does - and I'll pass it to you, Weapons Master - and there will be no more debating about it. There can't be any fooling with this one, it's too darned important. In a standup battle, either Claradon or I could lead, but that's not what we have. There's something queer about this whole business, what with the wailing and the circle and such. It's just not natural, not natural at all. It stinks of sorcery and the like. In this, the only man amongst us that has the experience to lead is Gabriel. He must take command."

"I agree," said Claradon as he turned toward the Weapons Master. "You can handle this much better than me. You must lead us. I don't have the experience."

Gabriel stared down at the table for several seconds. "For good or ill, it's your place to lead us Claradon, not mine. But Ob's points are well taken; Aradon's life may depend on our course, for that reason only will I agree to this."

He stood up. "We'll take a full squadron of knights. Ob, you will choose them and captain the squadron. Be sure to include Glimador, and Indigo, they're amongst my best students. And my squire and sergeant shall accompany us. The rest of the garrison will remain to defend the Dor. Par Tanch, you'll come with us of course."

Par Tanch's face blanched.

"Ector," said Gabriel, "If there's no word from us by midday on the morrow, you will send word to Lomion, Kern, and Doriath Forest, asking them each for aid. You will also send scouts to each town and hamlet within our demesne, instructing them to prepare for battle or to flee to Lomion or to the Dor. Understood?"

"Understood," said Ector.

"Perhaps I should stay behind and assist young Master Ector," said Tanch. "What with my delicate back and such I may not be—"

"We need your skills, wizard," said Gabriel. "You're going."

Tanch slumped back in defeat.

Gabriel's gaze, and then everyone else's, shifted toward the two foreigners.

"I'll accompany you," said Lord Theta before any could address him, "and Dolan as well."

"I thank you, Lord Theta," said Claradon, "but this isn't your fight. Don't feel obligated."

Theta cut Claradon off with a wave of his hand and a shake of his head. "I shall accompany you."

"Then you have my gratitude."

Theta nodded.

"Everyone, go now and make ready your equipment," said Gabriel. "We'll meet in the chapel in one hour."

III
ON MAGIC AND MUMMERY

As the men filed from the room, Theta motioned to Claradon to remain. He walked over as Theta gathered up his shield.

"Your wizard was reluctant to speak of magic," said Theta. "I would ask that you explain this."

"He behaved that way, because in Lomion it's considered rather improper to speak of such things. One reason being, most people believe magic is no more than mummery. The greater reason being, it's illegal to practice the true arcane arts publicly. Those that do so face ostracism at best, and prison or exile if things go against them. I gather that in your lands such is not the case."

"Indeed, things are different there. With your laws as they are, how is it that you have a House Wizard?"

"Ah, well- being a wizard, or rather, proclaiming yourself a wizard is not illegal. On every street corner in the great cities of the realm, there are those that call themselves wizards, sorcerers, or seers, but they are charlatans all. They trick the unwary and unwise with sleight of hand, and fool the foolish with palm readings, astrology, and other such bunk. As far as the common people know, that's all there is to magic and wizards. All that they know of true magic comes only from legend and superstition. We're a superstitious people you see, so the people fear those olden tales. They fear the olden magic and those that weave it. It's better to believe only in the card tricksters and their ilk."

"So they think our House Wizards are no more than well-dressed street hawkers."

"Exactly."

"And I gather that that isn't the case."

"Indeed, it is not. There are those few, those most singular few that belong to the Order of the Arcane. These men are learned in the true mysteries of the magical arts of thaumaturgy, divination, sorcery, necromancy, and other such esoteric fields of study. A goodly number of their members can command fantastic magics and enchantments to accomplish all manner of wondrous deeds. Par Talbon, our House Wizard, is such a man, as is Par Tanch. These men are sworn to never use their skills publicly, save in the defense of their lives, the lives of their master, or by order of the Crown. Rare it is that such vows are broken. When magic is used, the authorities quickly cover up the incidents and remove the evidence; the government long ago having decided that the common people mustn't know of such things. For good or ill, that's the way of things.

"And no one other than those in the Order can command the magical arts?"

"Some few members of certain militant orders are trained in the ways of magic. But their command of the arts is typically far more limited than members of the Arcane Order."

"I take it that these knights are under the same restrictions regarding using their arcane skills."

"They are."

"You have such skills," he said in a manner that could easily have been mistaken as a question – though it most certainly was a statement.

"I do," said Claradon, not quite holding back a slight grin at Theta's insight. "As you've no doubt already discerned, my brother and I are knights of the realm of Lomion, each holding membership in one of the militant orders. I serve the Caradonian Order of the Knights of Odin, and they afford me the title of 'Brother'. Ector and my brother Jude are members of the Tyrian Order, whose patron is Tyr, god of justice. Jude and Malcolm, my youngest brother, are in Lomion, our capital city, on House business."

IV
THE PRAYER

"Hear me my brothers," said Claradon as he stood beside the lectern, "now gather close and harken to my words, for they art passed down to us from the before time."

The assembled knights of Dor Eotrus dropped to one knee and bowed their heads. Lord Theta and Dolan stood alone in the rear of the chapel.

"Now look to the north and behold ancient Asgard, shining and bright, though hard and cold as the stone, the ice, and the sea."

"To the north lies Asgard," said the men in unison.

"Now look unto the east and behold thy brothers, thy sons, and thy comrades.

Now look unto the west and behold thy sisters, thy wives, thy mothers, and thy daughters."

"Around us are our kinsmen, always," said the men.

"Now think not again of them until we march on the homeward road."

"Not until the homeward road," said the men.

"Now look unto the south and behold thy father, and thy father's father, and all thy line afore thee, back unto the beginning."

"Unto the beginning," said the men.

"Now look forward and behold thy fate. For before you lay the paths to victory and glory, and the paths to defeat and disgrace. Intersecting these paths are the road to tomorrow, the road to Valhalla, and the road to darkness."

"Beware the dark road," said the men.

"Now look above thee and behold the all-father. He beckons us forth to meet our fate. He tells us that the path we choose is of our own making."

"Our path is our own," said the men.

"Now my brothers, vow thy path."

"We choose the path to victory and tomorrow if we can, to victory and Valhalla if we must," said the men. "This we vow."

"We shall bring Lord Eotrus home, or take vengeance on his slayers if he has fallen. This we vow."

"This we vow," said the men.

"Rise now my brothers," said Claradon, "and go to thy fate with Odin's blessing."

The men arose and stood silently for several moments.

"--All right, you slackers," bellowed Ob. "That's enough standing around. Check your weapons and secure your packs. We'll be heading out forthwith."

As the men prepared their equipment, Claradon moved to where Theta and Dolan were standing. "I hope that our rite did not offend or make you uncomfortable," he said, as he removed his clerical vestments.

"Not at all," said Theta.

"Vowing thy path," said Claradon, "is an ancient prayer amongst our people. We wouldn't embark on a quest or go off to battle without speaking it."

"We have a similar rite in our land," said Theta.

"Then why may I ask did you not join us and reaffirm your path?"

"I chose my path long ago, Eotrus. I know its every crag and crevice. I could no more divert from it, than could the sun choose not to rise in the morn."

"Then I'm glad that we'll face this road together, since you know it so well."

Theta stared off into the distance. "Mine is a perilous road; those that walk it with me are seldom long for Valhalla."

Dolan raised an eyebrow at this.

"Ominous words, my Lord," said Claradon. "I'd gladly end the day in Valhalla, if before I drew my last I avenged my father."

"Be not so quick to fly to Valhalla, young Eotrus, it will still be there however long your journey. It is…eternal."

V
DARGUS DAL

As the men adjusted their gear, Gabriel unlocked an ironbound chest that he and his aides had earlier dragged into the room. When he opened the lid, an unnatural glow crept from within. The men gathered about to get a closer look. Gabriel reached in and pulled forth a long dagger in a bejeweled leather sheath. When he bared the silvered blade, it glowed with a soft white light. Similar blades filled the chest.

The men gasped at the sight of that eldritch blade, ensorcelled as it was with some forgotten magic of bygone days to luminesce so. Most retreated several paces and some drew their swords.

"Sorcery!" said one knight.

"Witchcraft!" cried another.

"Hold," boomed Gabriel. 'There is no danger here. This blade and its kin are weapons for us to gird, not foes for us to fight. Cover your blades. Now."

The men complied, though fear and doubt filled many a face.

"What's this humbug, Gabe?" said Ob. "We've no need of fairy magics, we have honest steel to gird us."

"And honest steel is all one needs when facing mortal man or beast," said Gabriel. "But today I fear we face something more."

"Bah," said Ob.

"Sir Gabriel is right," said Par Tanch. "We're facing something whose howls carry for miles, that spouts evil fog and waylays our finest men. To face such an enemy, we need a bit of the arcane I think."

"Well, I'll have none of it," said Ob. "Nothing but rubbish."

"I'll not touch those things," said one knight.

"Nor will I," said another.

"I'll take one," said Claradon, as he and Theta moved toward Gabriel. Claradon reached out toward the glowing blade.

"Dargus dal is mine," said Gabriel as he sheathed it and reached down into the chest. "But you may have its twin." Gabriel pulled another wondrous blade from the chest and handed it to Claradon. "It's called Worfin dal, which means the lord's dagger in the old tongue."

"Asgardian daggers," said Theta. "I thought them all lost long ago."

"Not all, my Lord," said Gabriel. "Some few remain. I regret that I cannot offer you one, for of them I possess only two." He reached into the chest and withdrew another dagger. This one was longer and thinner than the first two. Its scabbard and pommel were less ornate, and although it glowed, its luminescence paled in comparison to the first two. He presented it to Theta.

"This one, and all the rest are of the finest Dyvers steel and ensorcelled by the arch-mages of the Order of the Arcane. No better blades are forged in Midgaard today, dwarven boasts notwithstanding."

Theta nodded his thanks.

"These blades will protect us from the baleful fog and blind our enemies with the light of just and valiant Tyr," said Gabriel. "There are enough for each of you. Each man will take one, like it as not. That includes you, good Castellan."

The men grumbled and grunted in protest, but in the end, each dutifully girded one of the daggers about their waist or ankle.

"I look forward to hearing the tale of how you acquired these," said Claradon.

"And I'll gladly tell it to you and Aradon both, upon our return."

"I'll be hearing that tale too," said Ob, "as long as it comes with mead or good gnomish ale."

VI
DOR EOTRUS

Claradon led the group from the central tower, the very heart of the Dor, through the courtyard and down Market Street, toward the main gates. As they made their way, they saw citizens dashing about, frightened looks etched on their faces. Many were carrying loads of food or other supplies, stocking up for a feared siege; some were loading wagons with all their worldly belongings, apparently preparing to flee the Dor for safer environs. More than a few residents of the Outer Dor, the town beyond the main walls, were filing into the keep proper, seeking more secure refuge for the night. There truly was an unmistakable and pervading sense of doom plaguing the keep. Dor Eotrus had ever been a place of strength, peace, and security. Now all that had changed.

Despite the circumstances, walking toward the main gates Claradon couldn't help but be impressed by the strength and majesty of the Dor itself. The twelve-foot thick outer and inner walls of the noble castle, crafted by master stonemasons, stood forty and sixty feet in height, respectively. Mammoth towers flanked the main gate and additional towers were situated at the four corners of both the outer and inner baileys. The towers' crenellated parapets partially obscured an array of large catapults and ballistae fortifying the roofs. Looking back, whence they came, he could see the enormous cylindrical tower they had recently exited. It was a magnificent work of engineering that approached two hundred fifty feet in height and included several majestic turrets and minarets that branched off from the primary tower.

Claradon had ordered the Dor's forces to prepare to defend against a possible attack and as they approached the main gate, he saw that the preparations were well underway. Squads of men-at-arms guarded the entranceway and the barbican area beyond. Soldiers on the allures were heating iron vats filled with oil and squads of crossbowmen stalked the battlements.

At the main gates, the men mounted fine horses and headed out. The guards bowed to Claradon as he passed. Several riders approached at a canter just as the group cleared the gates. Their leader pulled up alongside Gabriel and Ob.

"What news?" said Ob.

"No sign of the patrol, Castellan. We rode as far as five leagues into the wood. There were no animals,

THE GATEWAY

no birds, not even the sounds of insects. All life has fled the wood. I've never seen its like."

"Any sign of an enemy force?" said Gabriel.

"Or any strange beasties?" said Ob.

"None," said the scout.

The expedition soon passed through the Outer Dor and headed off the road, toward the Vermion Forest. Gabriel sent outriders to cover their flanks while Ob rode some ways ahead to scout. Gabriel rode at the vanguard of the main group, followed by his picked men. Behind them was Theta, Dolan, Par Tanch, and Claradon, the rest of the squadron closely followed.

As they rode through the ominous woodland, Lord Theta and Dolan conversed quietly. Dolan now looked little like a simple retainer; his aspect more akin to a veteran soldier or mercenary - donned as he was in a battered cuirass of brown and black-hued leather and equipped with a small arsenal of weaponry. He girded the well-oiled longsword sheathed at his side in the manner of a professional soldier, and the longbow engraved with strange pictograms that he wore over his shoulder was clearly oft used in battle. The hafts of several daggers protruded from sheaths at his boots and his shoulder.

"Lord Angle, after we've seen this business through, do you think perhaps we'll be able to go back home?"

Theta shrugged.

"I know we must be here for some reason, something big, more than just some strange goings on in some woods. We're not halfway 'round the world from home for just that. What do you expect we'll find in these woods, Lord Angle?"

Expressionless and even-toned, Theta replied, "Some world-eating monster or demon lord or ancient wyrm, no doubt. It matters not, for I will put it down whatever it be."

"I thought we took care of all of them fellas already?"

Theta ignored him.

"Guess there's some more lurking about. Never liked lurkers."

VII
THE CIRCLE OF DESOLATION

After two hours of travel through the darkened, foreboding forest the expedition came upon the dread circle of desolation. It was a bizarre and fearful sight. Not a single living thing existed across its stark and barren expanse. There was no foliage, animal life, or insect life whatsoever. The circle consisted of nothing more than a desolate, flat area of hardened soil that stretched out in a circular pattern several hundred yards in diameter. The edge curved out a perfectly smooth arc and was depressed several inches below the surrounding ground, such that one would have to step down to walk upon the circle's barren interior.

No enemies were about and the knights could discern no obvious signs of Lord Eotrus's patrol.

THE GATEWAY

Gabriel directed Ob to take two thirds of the squadron and scour the woodland beyond the unnatural circle. They were to search for signs of the patrol or of whatever enemy force had waylaid them. "But do not set foot within the circle until I give you leave," said Gabriel.

Meanwhile, the others examined the perimeter of the circle itself, none daring to venture beyond the rim after Gabriel's warning.

"We must determine whether it's safe step within," said Gabriel.

"Perhaps I can assist with that," said Par Tanch. "I think that the Arcane Order would approve the use of the sorcerous arts in this circumstance. So with your permission Sir Gabriel, I shall call upon my humble powers to divine if fell sorcery is at work here."

"Of course Par Tanch, have at it."

Par Tanch began his divination by chanting in a strange guttural tongue. He soon coupled his rather oppressive intonations with strange arm and hand movements, akin to a bizarre, primitive, and awkward dance. He tossed various sparkling powders about that gave off small bursts of light and puffs of smoke that smelled like rotten eggs. Such antics were mere mummery, and though wholly superfluous, the members of the Arcane Order seemed to think such things expected of them, so they carried on thus.

As Par Tanch put on his performance, Lord Theta quietly approached the rim of the circle several yards to the backs of the rest of the company. From a pouch at his belt, he produced an amulet inset with an oblong azure-hued gemstone that had the look of a sapphire, though it was actually a spinel. With this ancient charm, Theta could detect the presence or residues of all manner of arcane magics, marking them as either beneficent or fell. As he held it aloft and moved it toward the rim, the gem began to emit a soft flickering glow. The color of the stone quickly changed to a fiery red. As he passed his hand beyond the rim, the glow faded but did not extinguish.

Theta quickly replaced the amulet from whence it came, and then gripped the strangely twisted wooden ankh that hung from a leather cord about his neck. The ankh was no mere accouterment, but an ancient holy symbol preserved from some bygone age. One who grasped its deepest secrets could use it to detect the presence of certain maleficent creatures, beasts, or men. In its ear, Theta whispered words from ages past, forbidden words of power, long since lost to the world. Gripping the relic tightly, he surveyed the barren landscape before him. His eyes consumed the circle for several seconds, devouring every inch of it. Finally, he released the ankh, allowing it to fall back against his chest.

He then passed the tip of his lance across the rim of the circle and thrust it, gently at first, then more forcefully against the bleak soil within. He seemed to be testing the soil, as one might use a pole to probe the firmness of the ground when traveling through a swamp or bog.

Completing his ritual, Par Tanch cried, "Oh my, oh my. There is black sorcery at work here, Sir Gabriel. Fearful, insidious magic of a kind quite alien to me. I would say that--"

"Chaos sorcery lingers along the very rim," said Theta, as he moved to stand beside Tanch. "It emanates from something buried below the surface, but its power is waning."

Tanch raised an eyebrow at Theta's proclamations. The knights looked to Tanch, apparently skeptical of the conclusions of the foreign soldier.

"I agree with Lord Theta's most astute assessment," said Tanch. "I'd no idea you were so versed in the arcane arts, my Lord. To your assessment, I would add, however, that we can safely pass the threshold and enter the circle."

"I concur," said Theta. He boldly stepped across the rim and walked about to no ill effect.

"You men, break out the tools and try to uncover whatever is buried below the rim," said Gabriel.

VIII
CHAOS, COINS, AND CULTS

"How goes the work," said Tanch.

"Mr. Indigo's broken three shovels so far," said Dolan. "Mr. Paldor's only broken one. Not that he isn't trying as hard; it's just that he's smaller."

"This bloody ground's like frozen soil in the dead of winter," said Paldor.

"More like the packed dirt of an old road - in the frozen dead of winter," said Indigo as he wiped his brow with the back of his hand. "Not easy work."

"That much is clear," said Tanch. "Oh, I do wish I could assist you in your labors, but with my delicate back, I'm afraid such work is quite beyond me. Perhaps after I've rested a bit longer under yonder tree, I'll feel strong enough to heft the shovel for a time."

"Hold on." Look at what we got here," said Dolan as he lifted a shiny metallic object from the soil. "A gold coin with some strange markings."

Dolan passed it over to Tanch before redoubling his efforts to look for more.

The others gathered around as Tanch studied the coin for a time. "There's no doubt," said Tanch, "some strange arcane signature indeed emanates from this coin." He held out the coin toward Theta. "Would you care to examine it?"

Theta waved Tanch's hand away. He wouldn't touch the thing. Tanch held out the coin toward Claradon. "Master Claradon? Sir Gabriel?"

Claradon reached for the coin.

Gabriel started. "Stop!"

"Aie!" cried Claradon as he touched the coin, his face contorting in pain and revulsion. Gabriel swatted at Claradon's hand and the coin went flying. "

The darn thing burned my hand."

"It doesn't seem to like you Eotrus," said Theta chuckling.

"Are you hurt boy?" said Gabriel.

"It's a thing of evil! and should not be touched by a righteous knight," said Claradon, still wincing from the pain.

THE GATEWAY

"Oh my, oh my," said Tanch, hopping from one leg to the next. "I beg your pardon Master Claradon. I didn't know it would harm you. Please accept my deepest apologies. I didn't know. Truly, I had no idea that --"

"Tanch. Put the coin on that large stone," said Gabriel. "That way we can examine it without having to hold it up." Tanch did so.

"It's got many strange markings on its surface," said Dolan, still digging.

"They are mystical glyphs and symbols," said Tanch. He turned the coin over to view its obverse side.

"Mortach," said Theta.

"Indeed," said Tanch. "This symbol embossed on the surface is the mark of Mortach. The glyphs on the other side are used by Mortach's priests and followers for their vile rituals."

"Who's this Mortach fella?" said Dolan.

"He's a Chaos Lord," said Claradon.

"A who?" said Dolan.

"They are vile, maleficent, completely inhuman, otherworldly creatures," said Gabriel.

"Once they were men," said Theta.

"No longer," said Gabriel. "Now they are patrons of death, destruction, and all that is unholy and corrupt."

"Sorry I asked," said Dolan.

Gabriel continued, "They are few in number, but said to have lived since the dawn of time. They possess superhuman powers and wield incredible magics beyond the ken of even the greatest mortal wizards.

They are the sworn enemies of our lord Odin, and the rest of the beneficent gods of Asgard," the Aesir. "They reside on another world entirely, the very hell of myth and legend. There they command vast armies of lesser fiends, devils, demons, call them what you will."

"Legend has it," said Claradon, "that long ago these beings walked freely on our world," Midgaard, "but were driven off - back to their Courts of Chaos, by the great heroes of yore."

"Oh, now I get it," said Dolan. "We call them fellas 'Old Ones' back at home. Lord Angle and I don't get on well with them. You've a lot of them folks around here?"

"No, of course not," said Claradon. "If they were ever truly here, they are long since gone."

"But they're not forgotten on Midgaard," said Gabriel. "Even now, they're worshipped as gods by practitioners of the black arts— those schooled in the necromancy, demonology, chaos sorcery, and the like, and by other base individuals. These followers are murderers and lunatics all. They sacrifice innocents on unholy altars dedicated to the foul lords, in return for promised power, wealth, or more base desires. Cults of their followers are scattered here and there throughout all the known lands."

"They say that even in Lomion there's a secret temple dedicated to one of their number, Hecate, somewhere in the southeast section of the city," said Tanch. "Also—"

"--Here's another one," said Dolan, lifting a second golden coin out of the dense soil a few feet from where he had found the first. He passed it over to

THE GATEWAY

Tanch who placed it on the stone beside the first. Soon Dolan and the others had unearthed several more golden coins. They'd been uniformly spaced around the perimeter of the circle, buried some six inches down. Some bore the symbols of Mortach, as did the first, while others bore the symbols of Hecate. They recognized still other markings on some of the coins as symbols used by the priests of Bhaal, yet another chaos lord.

"It seems likely that these coins were enchanted by the followers of the chaos lords, and placed here by them for some as yet undetermined purpose," said Claradon, as they stood about the rock, studying the coins.

"I cannot explain it otherwise," said Gabriel. "So it seems we'll be going up against the followers of chaos, or some fell sorcery or some fiend or beast that they've conjured up." He paused for a few moments, and then turned to the rest of the group before continuing, "I will tell you that although it's not widely known, the followers of chaos have caused much suffering throughout Lomion over the years. The Crown and the Churches don't want such news causing panic so they've suppressed it. Few even know of the existence of these cults. But various covert military groups in Lomion, such as the Rangers' Guild and certain Church Knights, have battled against the cults a number of times. Ob and Artol and I have even had our troubles with them over the years. They're not to be trifled with. Unless they've taken our men prisoner in hopes of extorting a ransom, their involvement does not bode well for Lord Eotrus's safe return."

"Oh my. Oh dear," said Par Tanch. "We in the Order of the Arcane know of these fearsome cults as well. Going up against the followers of Bhaal or Mortach or Hecate is a serious thing. Going up against the cults of all three is tantamount to suicide. Their assassins have slaughtered many in their beds; still others have gone missing, never to be seen or heard from again. Perhaps we should reconsider this venture. Yes, perhaps we should go back to the Dor and get more men or better yet send for help from Lomion. Yes, clearly this is a job for the Lomerian army or the rangers of Doriath Hall. Clearly, this is much too dangerous for our small band. My delicate back just can't take the stress and exertion and --"

A wave of Gabriel's hand cut Tanch off. "Have you forgotten the nature of this mission, wizard?! We're here to help Lord Eotrus if we can, or to avenge his death if he has fallen. There's no reconsidering; we will do this thing."

Tanch's face reddened. "Of course, of course, we must press on and help Lord Eotrus," he said.

"Yes, we must," said Claradon.

"Please forgive me, I just meant to say that if there's fighting to be done I might not be able to help because of my delicate back." He put his arm behind his back and winced in pain to demonstrate his plight. "But we must press on. Indeed, indeed, we must, we must."

IX
MISTER KNOW-IT-ALL

After a time, having found nothing else of note within the circle, the men returned to the stone where they had placed the coins. Ob was already there, having completed his initial reconnaissance of the woods, and was examining the coins.

"Gabe," Ob called out, "we found tracks of Aradon's patrol."

Claradon's heart leapt to his throat at the gnome's words. Perhaps, there was some hope. He was anxious but fearful to hear what his gruff friend had to report.

"We found the patrol's tracks leading in from the east," from the direction of the Dor. "The tracks end at the rim of the circle, about fifty yards east of where we're standing."

They hurried over to where Ob had indicated, to see what there was to see.

"You see, these tracks," said Ob. "They get cut off right at the rim of the circle. No evidence they stopped or turned about. Someone must've blotted out the tracks."

"Or some thing," said Dolan.

"Oh my, I'm feeling faint," said Tanch. He leaned against Dolan for support.

Theta squatted down near the rim and studied the soil for some time.

"The number and age of the tracks makes them likely from Aradon's patrol," said Ob. "And here's the clincher, these shoeprints here are from Aradon's horse. It's a distinctive shoe; no other horse in the Dor has it."

Claradon knelt down to examine the print. "So, father was here. Now there's no doubt."

"The other patrols reported that the circle grew in size each night," said Gabriel. "That means that when Aradon's patrol was here, the circle was smaller. Since then, it must've grown and blotted out the tracks."

"But we still don't know how and why it's expanding," said Claradon.

"I found tracks from each of the other patrols too," said Ob. "Their tracks also end at the edge of the circle. But I found tracks from those patrols leading away from the area, returning back toward the Dor, which makes sense, since they made it home. There's no evidence of Aradon's patrol ever leaving, though. I couldn't find any tracks from his horses or his men leading away from the circle in any direction."

"But where could they have gone? How could they just vanish?"

"Maybe they got blotted, same as the tracks," said Dolan.

Theta cuffed him lightly on the back of the neck.

"Yow! Sorry boss."

"I don't rightly know, boy," said Ob. "I ain't ever seen the like of it. Glimador is doing another sweep of the area, but I think we found all that we're going to find. There's more to tell, though."

"We founded us a couple of black pillars a ways out over that way," pointing off to the west. "They're part of them ruins you talked of earlier, Gabe."

THE GATEWAY

"I knew we had to be close to the fell place," said Gabriel.

"I remember two pillars being about a quarter mile west from the old temple. Them pillars we found are the same two pillars. I'm sure about it."

"I remember those pillars," said Gabriel, "But that would put the main ruins –"

"- Right smack in the middle of that darn circle of nothing," said Ob.

"So the cult must've been using that old temple for some unholy rite of blackest magery," said Claradon. "But that still doesn't explain what happened to the temple ruins, or what this strange circle is about. Stone temples, even ruined ones, don't just disappear into thin air. Even masters of the arcane arts cannot easily accomplish such feats, I think."

"Perhaps their magic went awry, and the temple was somehow destroyed," said Tanch.

"Could the circle of coins be used to conjure up something, wizard?" said Theta. "Something from another world; something from the very Courts of Chaos themselves?"

"Perhaps, perhaps, but I cannot be sure," said Tanch. "Powerful chaos sorcerers have been known to possess the skills required to summon fiends from the beyond to do their bidding. But this circle, it's so vast, so enormous - far larger than you'd need for calling up some fiend or familiar. It must have some other purpose."

"Maybe they were conjuring something really big," said Dolan. He glanced sidelong at Theta, preparing to duck.

"I shudder to think of what such a thing could be," said Tanch. "No, I'm quite sure that their magic must have gone awry and caused the destruction of the temple and the formation of the circle."

"What if they were trying to conjure up one of them chaos fellas you told of Brother Claradon?" said Dolan as he edged farther from his master.

"It's hard to imagine such a thing being possible. Even if it were, the cultists would have to be mad to even attempt such a thing."

"Nevertheless, the circle is here," said Theta.

"Respectfully, sir, I don't think such a thing is possible," said Par Tanch. "You see, despite the colorful myths, these Chaos Lords aren't really men at all, they're more akin to forces of nature. The scholarly texts imply that they're beings of energy and thought, not mortal flesh. They couldn't really walk our world. No, the circle must be here for some other purpose."

"I wonder," said Claradon, "if perhaps they could change their form, taking on a form akin to a mortal body, becoming some type of avatar. Perhaps, in such a guise they could enter Midgaard, through some mystical portal or gateway."

"Such a theory would reconcile the ancient texts with the folk stories we've all heard, but"—

"Those are nothing but fairy stories, told to scare children," said Ob. "There's no truth to them. These chaos bozos are nothing but figments."

THE GATEWAY

"Let's pray that's the case," said Par Tanch. "For if a Chaos Lord did cross over to Midgaard, the entire world would be at utmost peril. Such a fiend would rampage across the land, leaving nothing but death and destruction in its wake. No mortal man, be he arch-wizard or knight champion could defeat such a beast."

"I would defeat it," said Theta in an even tone, almost but not quite under his breath.

"Bah!" spouted Ob. "You pompous tin can."

Theta glared at the gnome, but did not respond.

"Did you find anything else, Ob?" said Claradon.

"Yep, we did. We founded us some other tracks outside the circle. Wagon tracks, and horse spoor they was. The wagon was a big one, heavily laden with something or other, cause it sunk deep into the sod. Eight to ten horses rode with the wagon. All the tracks head south."

"Toward Lomion," said Tanch.

"Whoever they were, they'd set a camp out there by them two big pillars. But the signs point to them having left three or four days ago."

"So they would've been gone long before father's patrol arrived," said Claradon.

"That's right. So whoever they were, they weren't the ones that fought with the patrol," said Ob. "I checked the tracks; the horses' shoes didn't have no markings, so they didn't belong to any of the noble houses, the temples, or the guilds. So we don't know who they are."

"We should question them, if nothing else," said Tanch.

"Hell, we should track the bastards down and bust their heads, cause for sure, they know something."

"If need be, we can head after them on the morrow," said Gabriel.

"Even then we may catch them," said Ob. "They won't be making much time pulling a big wagon through this wild. They must be dumb as rocks to take a wagon in here. Nobody like that could've outsmarted Aradon."

"Maybe them folks with the wagon needed some stones, so they hauled the ruins away," said Dolan.

Theta grinned despite himself.

The other knights returned shortly, confirming that no tracks of Lord Eotrus's party led away from the circle of desolation. The patrol had not left there, at least not by any normal means. There was nothing else for the expedition to do, save to await the coming of the unnatural fog and to see what it brought with it. The men moved to set a camp in the wood, not far from where they had dug up the golden coins.

"Mr. Claradon," said Dolan, "you should try and eat a bit more than just bread. It's still a few hours until we expect the fog; you need to keep up your strength."

"I can barely manage the bread. I chew it and chew it, but without the water it won't go down."

"Nerves is normal, boy," said Ob as he chewed on a piece of jerky. "I'm worried about your father too, but we need to be at our best when we face whatever's to come."

"I know. You're right. I'm afraid if I eat more, I'll just end up spewing it back up."

"Spew at them chaos fellas," said Dolan. "That'll teach them."

Claradon and Ob both let out a chuckle.

"Claradon, me boy, I've known your father all his life, and his father afore him. He's as tough as nails, and a right fine swordsman. He'll be all right, I'm sure. We just have to believe that. That's all we can do for now."

Claradon nodded slightly in response as he stared over toward the edge of the circle.

"What're you looking at?" Ob turned around to see. Gabriel and Theta were standing watch together at the rim.

"I was just wondering what they're talking about," said Claradon. "Lord Theta doesn't seem to say much, but has much to say. Dolan, is he always like that?"

"Mostly," said Dolan, as he pulled some carefully packaged salted pork from his pack. "They say he's an enigma. I don't rightly know what that means, but they don't say it to his face, so it must be something bad."

"There's worse things to be, I expect," said Ob, as he too fixed his gaze on Theta. "That's quite a suit of armor your boss has, sonny," said Ob. "Why, it's as fancy and shiny as the ceremonial armor of ole King Tenzivel himself."

"It should be. I keep it well polished and bang out all the dents. There always seems to be more dents."

"Hmm. It sure is mighty pretty, but I'm a wondering if it can stand up to cold hard steel, or beasties' claws. Myself, I wouldn't wear no fairy armor like that in any case. No offense."

"None taken. But I wouldn't say that to Lord Angle, if I were you," he said, finishing off a piece of pork. "If you think his armor's fancy, you should see his castle – what with the weapon and trophy collections, the paintings, and all those fancy wines."

"Has his own castle does he?" said Ob. "He must be some important fella over there cross the sea where youse hail from."

"That he is. He's a brave hero," said Dolan matter-of-factly.

"You don't say?" said Claradon.

"Now sonny, just what has that fella done that makes him a hero?" said Ob.

"He's the kind that slays dragons, giants, monsters and such. Saved the world several times since I've been with him. They say he even fought the old gods way back in olden days, but I wasn't around then."

"Ho, ho. I see you're a teller of tales Dolan me boy," said Ob, chuckling. "Killing dragons, fighting gods, ho ho. I'd bet them's some goodly yarns to pass a cold night on the trail."

Dolan furrowed his brow and shook his head as he stared at another piece of jerky.

"He seems a man of courage and strength," said Claradon.

"He's stronger than any man I've ever seen," said Dolan. "Why there was that time--"

THE GATEWAY

"Bah," said Ob. "Me boy Gabriel there," gesturing toward him, "smashes beasties afore breakfast. He be a true hero, not some fancy dressed dandy wearing a tin can and having a pole up his behind. He got his reputation on the battlefield, not in some children's tales."

"That's true enough," said Claradon, as he looked toward Dolan. "More than twenty years ago, Sir Gabriel single-handedly slew a fire wyrm that was plaguing the villages of the Kronar Mountains. Later, he served as the Preceptor of the Order of the Knights of Tyr for several years before taking up service with my father. Many consider him the finest swordsman and Weapons Master in all Lomion. He –"

"And the only ones what don't think Gabe's the best is dumb or dead or both," said Ob. "And as for strong, just look at him," he said, pointing toward Gabriel, "He could squash that mister foreign fancy pants like a bug."

"I doubt that," said Dolan, narrowing his eyes at the crusty gnome.

"Bah," spouted Ob before taking a long swill from his wineskin. "I'd fancy a sample of them wines you mentioned though. I suppose if he likes a good bottle, he can't be all bad."

"I thank the gods Sir Gabriel is with us in this," said Claradon. "If he hadn't returned from hunting, if we had to do this without him…" Claradon shook his head, and closed his eyes tightly for a moment. Then he tried to down a bite of the jerky.

Though Gabriel had only served House Eotrus for the past ten years, he had made his mark on

Claradon's upbringing and his life. Of all the great men that Claradon knew, Gabriel was the one he yearned most to be like, the one whom he endeavored to model himself after. Where Aradon was his beloved father, Ob his closest friend, confidant, and lore master, Sir Gabriel was his hero. Where his father's book learning and Ob's vast experience about the realms had brought them great knowledge and wisdom, Gabriel far surpassed them. There seemed to be nothing he didn't know, nowhere he hadn't been. Where his father was a great swordsman with few peers in all the land, even his skills paled in comparison with Gabriel's. Verily, Gabriel could best any five knights of the Dor at once in mock combat; such was his skill. When Sir Gabriel spoke to a group of men, even those that didn't know him, he had no need to shout above them to gather their attention. The moment he uttered a word, all would become silent; everyone wanted to hear his words. Perhaps, it was due to the stories about him - his slaying of the fire wyrm, his defeat of the barrow-wight, his routing of the lugron horde, or any of the myriad tales that abounded of him, or perhaps, it was merely his regal bearing and commanding presence. Why a man such as he, who had the strength, talent, and knowledge to carve out an empire for himself would be content to serve as Weapons Master of a border fortress, Claradon could never fathom. When he asked him one day, Gabriel said that he had his reasons, but would speak no more about it.

After a time, Ob grew curious, as gnomes are often wont to do. "Come on boy. Let's go and see what

THE GATEWAY

them two is up to." Ob, Dolan, and Claradon rose and joined the two knights at the rim. Theta and Gabriel looked over at the three as they approached, hesitating only a moment before continuing their conversation.

"Do you sense it, my Lord?" said Gabriel.

"I do," said Theta, "I thought you might also."

"This be a truly unnatural place; and it's more than just this strange magical circle," said Gabriel. "There was great evil here recently; it comes with the fog I suspect."

"You are correct. When the fog returns, creatures not of this world will return with it."

"Gabe and me have fought such creatures afore a time or two over the years," said Ob. "Once over in the Dead Fens, another time in Southeast. I expect you have also, you being such a big hero and all."

"I have, many times," said Theta, peering down at the bellicose gnome.

"But these others have not," said Gabriel, gesturing toward the encampment. "They're fine soldiers, but they've no idea what terrors await them here this eve."

"They will learn, or they will die. Such is the way of things," said Theta.

"A regular ray of sunshine, aren't you Theta?" said Ob.

"Put your teeth together, gnome, and open your ears," said Theta. "This place – it's even more sinister than I think you realize. It's becoming a gateway, a portal, to a place more horrific than any mortal can imagine - a place of incomprehensible evil, of mind shattering idiotic chaos, of pure insanity. Those who dwell there, beyond the pale, would make this place like that. This is what we must prevent. This is why we are here. We must seal this gateway, forever. This is our true quest."

Ob's mouth dropped open at these words and he stared at Theta in disbelief. Gabriel merely stoically nodded his agreement. Theta's words so shocked Claradon he could say nothing.

"What are you about, Theta?" said Ob. "Portal to another world? What madness is this? Listen young fella, I know you wouldn't guess it from looking at me pretty face, but I'm three hundred and sixteen year old and have been from one side of this continent to the other more times than you've had birthday's, and I've never seen nor heard tell of such a thing. Sure, there be some powerful wizards what can conjure up a strange beastie or two, but nothing more. Gateway to another world, bah."

Theta responded in a smooth and level tone, "Nevertheless, what I've said is true." Just a hint of anger could be detected in the set of his jaw and slight furl in his brow. "I will prevent the gateway from opening or close it once it does. You men can assist or not – it matters little to me. I will do what needs to be done."

"Bah! Mr. Know-it-All," said Ob. "You're nothing but a boaster and a braggart with no true mettle. Theta, if some creature from another world be coming at you, I'd bet you'd soil that fancy armor of yours in a heartbeat. Hell, you'd be down on your knees begging for mercy, pleading for your life, or running away with your tail between your legs!"

THE GATEWAY

"Enough! Ob." said Gabriel. "Lord Theta is here to help us, not to be insulted by a loudmouthed gnome. I'll hear no more of it."

"I think what I think, and I'll say what I say, and if anybody don't like it, they can stuff it," spat the gnome.

"Lord Theta," said Claradon, "perhaps you could explain your reasoning regarding this gateway, you mentioned? What is it that you think is really going on out here?"

He paused and took a slow deep breath before responding. "It's what we were discussing afore. I believe followers of the chaos lords are using the arcane properties of this eldritch place, the ancient temple and the other ruins that were here, and their own fell sorceries, to open a gateway to the very Courts of Chaos. Verily, when that happens, all hell will come through - literally. It would mean the end of civilization. The end of everything we all hold dear."

"But why do you think this? All we've seen here is an empty circle, a few golden coins, and some tracks, nothing more."

"Because I've seen such things afore, in times past, and because of the demon spoor polluting this place." He pointed toward the smooth, stony soil. "The tracks in the circle."

"You're daft, man," said Ob. "I told you, there be no tracks there. The only tracks we've seen are outside the circle, and they're just tracks of men and horses. You're just spouting some more of your fairy stories." He took a swig from his wineskin.

"Look again, gnome," said Theta with an even tone, as he pointed toward the ground within the circle. "Perhaps you were blinded by the forest and failed to see the trees."

"What?" said Ob, turning toward Claradon with a bewildered expression. "I don't understand this fella. He talks all funny."

"Maybe you should have another look," said Claradon.

"Last I checked I was Master Scout of the Dor, bucko," said Ob sternly. "Nobody can read tracks better than me – not rangers, not stinking elves, and certainly not no tin cans. But I'll have another gander, just to settle this business once and for all." Ob got down on his hands and knees at the rim of the circle and peered down, carefully studying the ground.

Theta squatted down next to him. "There, and there," he said, gesturing toward some small features on the surface of the hardened soil. "And there and there," he pointed. Ob studied the ground, moving about over a small area, and poking some at the soil. This went on for some time. When he finally stood up and turned towards the others, his face was ashen and contorted in a look of shock and bewilderment.

"I cannot hardly believe what I've seen. I missed it afore, I missed it entirely," he said, shaking his head in disgust.

"What did you miss Ob?" said Claradon. "Are there tracks there or not?"

"Theta's been speaking the truth, about the tracks at least. There be tracks all right. There be nothing but tracks, which is why I missed them afore.

THE GATEWAY

That ground, it's been stamped down and compressed by a thousand thousand feet walking over and over it. The tracks are so overlapped; they obscure each other almost completely, making them appear not to be tracks at all. But they are -I'm sure of it now. And they're not people tracks or the tracks of some animal neither. They're the tracks of some type of beastie, some type of monster like I've never seen afore."

"How do you know that?" said Claradon.

Ob held out his palm and displayed an object that he had pulled from the soil. It was a claw - pitch black, more than nine inches long and nearly three inches wide.

Blood dripped from Ob's hand. "It's razor sharp," he said. "And look at the size of it. No natural beast has such a claw."

"Gods," said Claradon. "It must've broken off some creature, some monstrosity, some thing from the hell Lord Theta spoke of."

"All right, Theta," said Ob. "So how do we seal this gateway?"

"When the fog comes, we'll find a way," said Theta. "There's always a way."

"Find a way?! What the heck kind of plan is that?" said Ob. "And what-- and what of Aradon?"

Theta looked toward Claradon before responding. "He and his men are dead. Of this, I have no doubt."

Claradon's throat tightened up and his hands grew icy cold as he realized the truth of Theta's words. Gabriel put an arm around his shoulders. "We'll get through this," he said quietly.

"How do you know all these things?" said Ob. "Who are you, Theta? Who are you really?"

Lord Theta turned and began to walk away. "Perhaps tonight you'll find out."

Ob's weathered visage blanched at Theta's ominous words. Gabriel, Ob, Dolan, and Claradon watched the mysterious knight walk back toward the makeshift encampment.

"Should we tell the men?" said Claradon.

"What would you have me tell them?" said Gabriel. "That the world is ending?"

Claradon shrugged.

"That we've a madman amongst us," said Ob. "He'll be the doom of us all. Stinking foreigners."

"You're the stinky one," said Dolan wrinkling his nose, and then following after Theta.

X
THE FOG

Not long before midnight, the moonlight revealed a small area of fog forming at the center of the zone of desolation. There was no fog anywhere else about, only there at the circle's center, and it was forming fast; too fast for something natural.

"Make ready!" shouted Ob.

The men scrambled to their feet.

An unnatural wind sprang up and the fog rapidly expanded radially outward, rolling toward them like a giant wave.

THE GATEWAY

"Form up, men," shouted Sir Gabriel. "Tight formation! Shield wall! Shield wall!"

"Draw your weapons men, and make ready," boomed Ob.

The men rushed together, and aligned shoulder to shoulder, four rows deep, in expert fashion. In moments, they were ready. The front row held tower shields tightly together. The second row held pikes.

"This is it," said Dolan, a smile on his face. "Mr. Claradon, get ready to spew."

Claradon felt near ready to comply.

In moments, the eerie cloud filled the entire circle, but expanded nary an inch beyond its rim. Standing just there, the expedition was untouched by the foul vapors. No one dared move; they barely breathed. Moments passed that seemed like hours whilst they looked and listened for some sign of their enemies. But there was nothing.

A second gust of wind and the fogbank expanded again, swallowing the whole of the expedition within its maw. The men suddenly felt lightheaded and nauseous as the diabolical fog settled around them, clinging to their flesh, threatening to rend it from their very bones. The foul mist even stung their eyes, blinding them. The temperature plunged instantly to well below freezing, chilling them to the bone and sapping their strength. A strange bestial odor filled the air.

"What is this, what's going on?" shouted one knight.

"Tis some evil magic" said a second knight.

"I feel ill," said another. "My head swims."

"And mine," said several others.

"Black Sorcery it is," called out one man.

"Devil's work," said another.

"Steady men," shouted Ob, "remember your training."

"Hold your formation," boomed Sir Gabriel.

Soon, their vision cleared, but the thickness of the vaporous stuff was such that one could scarcely see ten feet ahead.

Theta moved from his position in the line and boldly advanced into the preternatural fog, lance in hand, with nary a word or glance to any. Dolan scrambled to follow his liege.

"Draw the daggers I gave you and follow Theta," commanded Sir Gabriel.

"Steady boys and forward," shouted Ob. "And for Tyr's sake, stay together. I'll not be searching the fog for you."

The warriors caught up to Theta about a hundred yards into the fogbank. He was standing amidst a killing field. The mutilated corpses of more than a dozen men littered the ground where minutes before there was nothing. It was the missing patrol. How the bodies appeared there, they could not fathom. Each corpse was horribly desecrated in unspeakable ways; ways which should not be described save to say that the remains could only be identified by fragments of their armor, shields, and clothing.

Claradon made to approach.

"Get back boy!" said Ob, as he interposed himself between the young knight and the grisly remains.

THE GATEWAY

"You don't want to see this." Ob grabbed him tightly by the arm to hold him back.

"Stand aside. I have to see."

"No you don't," said Ob. "You don't want to remember him this way."

Claradon shoved him aside and moved forward.

"Dead gods," said Claradon, as he drew close. "Dead gods," was all he could utter. Claradon's eyes welled with tears, try as he could to prevent it.

"What could do this to a man?" said Ob to Gabriel.

Gabriel shook his head, and looked away.

Despite the terrible chill, some of the knights reverently placed their cloaks over the fallen. The men gathered around, and bowed their heads as Claradon spoke a short prayer to Odin.

"We cannot linger here," said Ob. "We'll be giving them a proper burial when the night's work is done. Then there'll be time to grieve. Now there's not. Now we've enemies to find and to kill."

"Now is the time for vengeance," shouted Claradon. "For retribution!"

"Vengeance!" shouted the men.

Claradon picked up his shield and adjusted his helm, wondering whether they'd all end up dead before the night was done. But Sir Gabriel was with him, *thank the gods. He's never been beaten. He can't be defeated. I'll stay at his side and make it through this. My path is to victory and tomorrow.* "To victory and tomorrow," he shouted.

"To victory and tomorrow!" shouted the men as they resumed their progress, deeper into the fog.

"We will find whoever did this," said Claradon. "For them, there will be no escape."

Gabriel and Claradon joined Theta at the vanguard of the group. The three advanced as one, Theta in the center. Soon they came upon a mammoth, black stone building. It was directly in the center of the fogbank, where nothing had been only minutes before. Blacker than anything natural, it absorbed all light, even that of Gabriel's mystical daggers. This and the dense fog prevented the men from discerning the true shape and full extent of the sinister edifice. At the front of the structure were six black steps that led up to a raised landing. Atop the landing were six cylindrical columns of the same black stone. The tops of the columns, lost in the fog, presumably supported some type of canopy far above. Climbing the strange black steps, the feelings of lightheadedness and nausea returned, more powerfully this time. Claradon forced himself onward despite his swimming head and churning stomach.

As he reached the top step, he turned and faced the men. Through the fog, he gazed upon a sea of shining helmets lined up three abreast. The biting cold of the place assaulted him. Through chattering teeth, he shouted, "The guiding light of just Tyr shall preserve us, men. And we shall have our rightful vengeance!"

"For House Eotrus," shouted the men.

Claradon realized his mistake after catching Theta's withering glare and hearing the growls from Ob and Gabriel behind him.

"Let's pipe down and keep moving men," said Gabriel.

"Yeah, there may still be some beasties way in the back that haven't heard us coming yet," said Ob. "Maybe we should take up a tune, so we won't startle them."

XI
THE TEMPLE OF CHAOS

They proceeded across the front landing and came upon a large pair of black stone doors. Theta gripped the huge bronze handles and pulled. Though there was no visible lock or bar, the doors didn't budge. Before Gabriel and Claradon could move to assist him, he pulled again, this time seeming to strain somewhat with the effort. Thundering crunching and cracking sounds emanated from the doors and the whole landing vibrated, threatening to collapse around them. The men scattered.

Suddenly, the doors shattered and began to crumble to pieces, Theta's mighty grip having literally ripped them asunder. The stony remains fell in heaps about the entranceway, the two bronze handles remaining in Theta's iron grip.

"Damned showoff," said Ob. "They was probably about to fall apart on their own, anyways. Bad workmanship, probably elvish."

Theta peered inside for a few moments, then stepped over the rubble and stalked cautiously into the malevolent stone edifice. The rest followed, weapons bare. Strangely, it was even colder inside than without, though the mist was thinner. The air, oddly thick and heavy, had a curious, acrid taste. The same bestial odor resided here, as outside, only stronger.

Theta removed one small object and then another from his belt pouch. He tossed one to each side of the darkened hall. The objects shattered, and then somehow illuminated much of the place. The men gasped at this bizarre phenomenon and gazed warily at the foreign knight. The mysterious lights were bright and strong for a few moments, then they grew softer and dimmer as the foul blackness of the place devoured them, turning all to shadow. The light didn't wane entirely; enough remained for the men to see.

The structure's interior was a most singular hall, some sixty feet in width, stretching into the darkness beyond the limits of the men's vision. The size and scale of the place were all wrong. It was too massive, too ponderous, and too meticulous to have been man-made in the days of yore. It featured two rows of massive, ornate, obsidian columns set thirty feet apart, forming a wide corridor extending from the entranceway toward the rear of the foreboding structure. The ceiling, lost in the darkness, surely resided more than fifty feet above. The flagstones were ground perfectly smooth; the joints between them so flawlessly cut and fitted as to require no mortar. Expert craftsman, possessing skills far beyond those of the most renowned of modern masons or artisans had built this place. Surely, the Old Ones or their minions - those ancient fiends that walked Midgaard before the

THE GATEWAY

dawn of man, had constructed it. Somehow, the fell sorcery at work here had restored the antediluvian temple, which had only lately been no more than a crumbling ruin, to all its former majesty and fearful glory.

The men stalked into the sinister structure, their way illuminated by Theta's magic, and by the soft white light emitted by their mystical daggers. From the moment they entered that place, it seemed to Claradon that everything moved in slow motion. Perhaps it was the dizziness and nausea afflicting him, perhaps something more. Even his boots made ominous, echoing sounds as he crossed the strange black stones. Unnaturally loud they were - the mystical nature of the edifice serving to amplify the sound tenfold.

At Gabriel's direction, they fanned out and began to move deeper into the black hall. As they did so, a bizarre, inhuman wailing sprang up all around them, emanating from the very walls themselves. The men halted, weapons held at the ready.

"What madness is this?" said one knight.

"Where is the sound coming from? I can't see them," shouted another.

"Steady boys," said Ob, "keep moving forward, the sounds can't hurt you."

As they moved inward, the shrill wailing increased. Growling, malefic intonations began: roaring and barking, howling, chattering, and gibbering. No throat of man or beast could produce the bizarre cacophony that filled that evil place. It surely sprang from the demonic tongues of a thousand wretched fiends reveling in the very pits of hell itself.

The faces of the brave knights blanched as the skirling sounds oppressed them and the bitter cold within the place took hold. They were soldiers, schooled in battle and tactics. They knew how to fight as a unit, or duel in single combat. But this was altogether different. An unseen enemy, whose caterwauling could deafen and disorientate - this was beyond their experience, beyond their training. All they could do was flee or follow their officers' orders and move forward against the din. They followed orders.

As they approached the first line of obsidian columns, the grotesque, debased, painted bas-reliefs adorning their surfaces came into view. Every manner of horrific, depraved, obscene, and unspeakable activity was prominently, even proudly, depicted on the gruesome faces of those sinister pillars. Such was the horror of those odious images that the men surely would have lost their sanity, if not their very souls, had they gazed upon them for more than mere moments.

The hellish din continued to intensify and soon the walls of the vile edifice and the surfaces of the black pillars began to move and wriggle as if alive. Hideous pseudopods shaped like malformed hands, claws, and demonic arms began to push against and protrude from within the black stone. The obsidian surfaces seemingly transformed to nothing more than thin, opaque, elastic veils. The horrid appendages writhed and flailed about, seeking to ensnare the men as they moved past. This was madness, a fevered nightmare.

Claradon cringed as he thought of the hordes of fiends that struggled to burst through the flowing stone and enter the world of man from somewhere beyond the pale. The dim light and eerie shadows that filled the place only served to enhance the horror of the surreal scene and unnerve even the bravest of the company. Looking around at his comrades, Claradon saw stony resolve on the faces of some; stark terror marred the aspects of others. Steamy breath rose from all, as did the soft glow of the ensorcelled daggers.

Gabriel and Ob offered words of encouragement to keep the troops moving forward. Through the din though, most surely couldn't hear them. Lord Theta pressed on at the van, stalking cautiously forward, brandishing his silver lance like a spear while evading the writhing things protruding and shot out from the columns.

One of the knights was not so careful, however, and strayed too close. A snakelike appendage darted out and wrapped itself about the knight's waist, pinioning his arms. It effortlessly lifted and pulled him toward the column. Ob and Claradon dashed toward the struggling knight, but before they could reach him, another tentacle appeared from above and grasped the knight about the neck. The evil limbs pulled in opposite directions and ripped the man's head from his shoulders. Blood spurted in all directions, washing over Ob and Claradon, who gasped in horror at the monstrous sight. The vile tentacles quickly pulled back and disappeared to whence they came. Ob and

Claradon moved toward the column with swords raised, to deal out whatever vengeance they could.

"Stop," shouted Par Tanch from nearby. "Don't strike out at the things. You might break the seal and give them entry; then we'd surely be doomed." Mindful of the wizard's words, they wisely backpedaled from the column, moving beyond the range of the pseudopods.

"This is it. We're doomed. It's the end of the world," said Tanch. "I told you we should've sent for the army."

"Stow that talk you sniveling turd or I'll bash your knees in," said Ob. Ob raised his wineskin to his lips and took a long draught as he pressed forward.

Claradon's vision clouded and his stomach churned as the waves of nausea and lightheadedness flooded over him with renewed vigor. The abominable clangor increased to near deafening levels, threatening to implode his very skull. Time and space became increasingly distorted; everything moved slower and slower.

Blood began to stream from the men's noses and ears as the pressure and maddening cacophony intensified. Several of the knights doubled over and vomited great gobs of putrescent green ichor as the sinister forces of the place assailed their mortal bodies. Others simply collapsed unconscious to the ebony slab.

Claradon watched in horror as a claw-like pseudopod pushed out from a column and grabbed the ankle of one of the fallen knights. The soldier screamed in terror as it dragged him to his doom. Claradon was simply too far away to come to the poor man's aid. Those who were closer were either too dazed from the madness about them, or too shocked to spring to his rescue. The knight's magical dagger sent sparks flying everywhere as he repeatedly and ineffectually stabbed it into the obsidian slab, trying to slow his inevitable slide. Within seconds of reaching the pillar, other demonic pseudopods and misshapen hands fell upon him and tore him limb from limb.

"I can't take this noise, it's maddening," shouted one knight. "If we can't strike out at these things we must flee before we're all torn to pieces."

Ob grabbed him and pulled him forward, "You're a knight of Dor Eotrus, boy, and you'll not flee while I yet live, that's for certain. We face this together. Come on," he shouted as he steadied the knight and pressed forward. "For House Eotrus! To victory and tomorrow."

Tanch pressed his hands to his ears, trying to stop the maddening noise from reaching him. He must have attempted to recall some bit of magic, some arcane spell or charm, that could protect him from the din, but how could he focus his thoughts through that insane cacophony? Blood streamed from his nose and his eyes were unfocused. His strength sapped, he collapsed to his knees. Even Ob staggered and fell, his gnomish ears being particularly susceptible to the horrific emanations.

Claradon focused his concentration as best he could and through chattering teeth bespoke the mystical words that called forth the power of Odin. A brilliant white light appeared and encompassed him. This mantle of holy light served to diminish the deafening sounds and the spatial distortions occurring directly around him, and would safeguard him from the claws and fangs of any creature of chaos that might appear. Alas, his power was not nearly great enough to encompass and aid his comrades. Already weakened, however, he could do little more than hold his ground.

At the far end of the hall, Claradon saw the temple's adytum - a black stone table, an unholy altar no doubt to the foulest fiends of chaos. Its surface was covered in deep reddish stains; the dried blood of untold innocents, spilled to sate the unquenchable thirsts of unspeakable outré beings.

Behind the altar, the rear wall of the temple was embossed with a strange pattern of circles within circles. At the center of the pattern was a gaping black hole of nothingness, a void. To where it led, man was surely not meant to fathom. The radius of each of the circles was twice that of the circle within it. The lines forming the five innermost circles were blackened and charred as if they had burned away - only moldering gray ash remained. Within these circles, inscribed in a dark red pigment - which surely was human blood - were all manner of arcane runes and eldritch symbols from the bizarre lexicon of some otherworldly fiends, forgotten gods, or mad arch-mages.

The sixth or outermost circle was glowing and burning a fiery red; the very flames of hell itself danced and writhed on its unholy surface. The space between the fifth and sixth circles was filled with twins of those curious golden coins, evenly spaced about the circle's circumference. Surely, when the sixth circle burned through, there would be no holding

THE GATEWAY

back the foul tide that was to come - the very armies of insanity and chaos, the maleficent denizens of the pit.

Even now, the rear wall, etched with the unholy pattern, bulged and flexed and flowed, ready to burst from the pressure of some massive monstrosities straining against its far side. In moments they would burst through - the beasts from beyond would walk once again on the world of man and usher in mankind's doom.

Sir Gabriel pressed onward toward the black altar followed by his towering, red-bearded sergeant, Sir Artol. Artol was unstopped by the maddening chaos, perhaps somewhat protected by his thickly padded steel helm if not his thick skull, but blood flowed freely from his nose, mouth, and even his eyes. Sir Miden staggered just behind them, valiantly trying to press forward though blood gushed from his nose and mouth. Overcome by the pain, Miden dropped his sword and shield, ripped off his helm, and clasped his hands to his ears to stave off the intolerable sounds and pressure. Just as he seemed to recover a bit and began to step forward, his entire head erupted in fountains of blood and gobs of gore that went spouting in all directions. His body swayed for a moment before collapsing in a heap.

Claradon couldn't believe his eyes. He threw more of his energy to the mystical mantle that shielded him.

At the sight of poor Sir Miden's fate, several knights turned and fled the temple in terror. Their loyalty to House Eotrus was without question, but this madness was too much. There was no enemy to smite here, no honor or glory to be gained, no vengeance to be had, only mindless suffering and senseless death. They'd had enough. They fled. A few even dropped their swords or shields in their haste to escape. Ob's commands and curses at them went unheard and unheeded in the chaotic din.

Claradon watched them flee. *This can't be real. It must be some vile nightmare. It can't truly be happening.*

Lord Theta seemed less effected by the evil phenomenon than were the others. No blood flowed from him and his eyes remained focused. His face, however, turned bright red and his stride slowed nearly to a crawl. He trudged forward in slow motion, several yards ahead of Gabriel, laboring as if dragging a great weight. At last, he reached the altar and the source of the evil. A small orb of utter blackness and purest evil sat atop the ebony slab of the altar. Theta must have known it was the foul emanations of this unholy artifact that fueled the chaos about him. It was its power that threatened to open the gateway to the unspeakable realms beyond the pale - the very Courts of Chaos themselves. Theta dropped his lance and pulled his war hammer from his belt. He raised it above his head with great speed, and then swung it down toward the orb with all his might.

Just before or perhaps just after his hammer hit home, the rear wall of the building gave way, emitting a massive blast of air and heat into the unholy temple. The explosion blasted Theta backward, hurtling him some forty feet before slamming him to the unyielding stone slab. Momentum propelled him several yards farther before mercifully releasing him. Though Theta surely took the brunt of the force, the blast knocked all the men from their feet.

Claradon looked over in horror at Theta's still form. *Another brave man dead, a mad nightmare this is.* Then he saw the six-foot wide hole in the temple's rear wall. Beyond the hole, was utter blackness - a portal to some other place, some other dimension, some foul bastion of chaos. The rim of the portal was aglow with wisps of yellow fire, their origin unknown. The arcane pattern's outermost circle was gone - its crimson border now nothing more than blackened and charred ash. The eldritch coins had melted and their remnants were trickling down the shattered wall in golden rivulets.

From out of that ominous hole, which proved indeed to be a gateway, raced a monster the like of which Claradon had never seen before, and until that very moment did not truly believe existed. It was an otherworldly creature of nightmare, of folklore; the very bogeyman of the children's tales come to life. The thing was a horrid caricature of a man. No flesh covered any part of the seven-foot tall creature's oversized skull. Its large red, glowing eyes and long forked tongue were alight with demonic flame. It wore strange black armor that clung tightly to its muscular torso. In its right hand it held a six-foot long white sword whose blade danced with red and yellow flame. Upon its massive breastplate was damasked the unmistakable symbol of the chaos lord Mortach. Could this hideous beast be the dread Lord Mortach itself, the mythical patron of death and destruction? Surely, any mortal who stood against such a fiend would be tossed aside like so much chaff. Before Claradon or his men could gain their feet, the creature sped through the hall and bounded out the entry – out into the world of man.

The unnatural pressure within the edifice was now gone and the earsplitting cacophony subsided. The pseudopods and tentacles retreated from the walls and columns and they returned to their normal stony aspects. Waves of heat and the noxious scent of brimstone now filled the air, emanating from the abyss beyond the breach. Behind these wafted a strong putrescence mixed with the bestial odor detected before.

As those who were still conscious staggered coughing and gasping to their feet, Claradon gazed in disbelief as more unspeakable horrors appeared. They rose through the rarefied ether of the abyss beyond the gateway by some bizarre means of locomotion incomprehensible to man. Several nightmarish creatures more than six feet tall and only roughly human shaped vaulted through the breach and entered the unholy temple. Their appearance was too monstrous, too ghastly to describe or even contemplate. No mortal creature ever possessed an aspect of such indescribable horror, such loathsome, abominable evil. Claradon shuddered as he looked upon the faces of pure chaos. As horrific as they were, they were beings of flesh and blood and sinew; Claradon and his comrades knew how to deal with such things.

Claradon, Sir Conrad, and Sir Martin were the first to rush forward, yelling battle cries to their

THE GATEWAY

patron gods Odin, Tyr, and Anarian. By the time they approached the gateway an even more formidable being had pushed the ghastly fiends aside. It was nearly eight feet tall and covered from head to toe with sharpened metallic spikes. It was brick red in color, except for its large eyes, which glowed a brilliant gold.

Claradon saw many more loathsome beasts pushing forward behind the spiked giant, striving to gain entry to the world of man. Verily, a veritable horde of hell was spewing forth from that malefic gateway to Abaddon. The spiked giant brandished a huge black sword and pointed it at the three knights.

"Bow down," it roared in the tongue of man, "Bow down petty creatures and pledge allegiance to Lord Gallis Korrgonn, Prince of Chaos, and son of almighty Azathoth. Bow down and swear fealty to me and I may spare your pathetic lives."

Claradon's whole body shuddered and quaked at the sight and sound of this unspeakable, nightmarish thing. He felt puny and naked. A paralysis washed over him, rooting him in place. He knew he was about to die. A Lord of Chaos was about to annihilate him.

He wanted to run. He wanted to hide. He wanted to scream. *If I just bow down, perhaps I might yet live. Such a little thing it would be, to just bow down. I could do this, couldn't I, to save my life? What harm would it do?*

He remembered his father. He remembered his burning need for vengeance.

He did not bow down. He would never bow down before any servant of chaos.

He would have his vengeance.

"I am Brother Claradon Eotrus, Lord of Dor Eotrus," he shouted.

"You killed my father; for this you die!"

Claradon charged forward; from the corners of his eyes, he saw that his two comrades were still with him. The smaller fiends sprang forward, interposing themselves between their dark lord and the knights.

"Very well, petty creatures," said Korrgonn. "We shall feast on your souls tonight. This world is ours now!"

The knights fought with incredible ferocity, their swords and strength against the claws and fangs of the hellish spawn of chaos. Outnumbered, the fiends pressed them back, away from the gateway and away from Korrgonn. Through the whirl of battle, Claradon was cut off from his comrades and fought on alone. The mantle of holy light that enshrouded him blinded the fiends and they shrank from it. Many turned from him and sought other victims. This gave him a singular advantage in the wild melee and perhaps was all that preserved his life. It also allowed him brief moments of respite during which he caught glimpses of the deadly struggles unfolding around him. Numerous devils attacked his still dazed or unconscious comrades and others engaged in duels to the death with the knights still standing. He saw Sir Bilson's throat ripped out by one fiend, and young Sir Paldor's chest slashed by another, but the brave knight fought on. Two fiends decapitated another knight and feasted on his corpse. Through the dim light, he spied Sirs Conrad and Martin, awash with blood and gore, pulled down and torn limb from limb by a group of bloodthirsty, multi-armed fiends. Then he saw Ob, fighting alone, darting here and there, evading the claws of the beasts, no doubt cursing all the while, several fiends stalking at his heels. It pained him that he could do nothing to aid his comrades. It was all he could do just to stay alive in the wild melee.

Tanch opened his eyes and pulled himself to a sitting position. Blood dripped from his nose and his eyes were unfocused. The bloody corpse of a fiend lay across his legs. Just to his left lay the corpse of one of Dor Eotrus's knights, his heart torn from his chest. A few feet away, Ob fought desperately with two fiends; several others already lay dead at his feet. Ob held a sword in one hand and a glowing dagger in the other and spun a wild dance of death about him; whirling, spinning, and darting to and fro in a manner impossible to believe for one of his age and stature. He thrust his sword through the breast of a fiend but it held fast as he tried to pull it out. As he struggled to withdraw it, he buried his short blade in the breast of the second fiend. From out of nowhere, another fiend appeared and clamped its devilish jaws upon Ob's forearm.

Ob wailed in agony but managed to stab the thing in the throat with his dagger. The beast fell back spouting ichor from its neck. Slumping back against one of the pillars, the wounded gnome struggled to wrap some cloth about his injured arm to stem the flow of his lifeblood. As Tanch watched in horror, a six-legged fiend with a vaguely batrachian aspect pounced on the tiny man. Par Tanch had only a moment to act.

"By the Shards of Pythagorus, gek paipcm ficcg," said Par Tanch. Six fist-sized spheres of blue fire appeared in the wizard's hand, one after another, and shot at the vile demon. The first bored into its left shoulder and exploded, the second detonated a few inches lower, blasting off the limb entirely. The third, fourth and fifth spheres punctured the creature's side and chest; the last blew a large chunk out of its bulbous head. Its corpse collapsed at Ob's feet.

Sirs Paldor, Glimador, and Indigo sprang to Ob's aid. The three soldiers interposed themselves between the devils and their wounded Castellan and held the fiends at bay.

XII
THE HERO'S PATH

The monstrous fiend, Korrgonn, strode up the hall toward the temple's entrance, stepping on as often as over the still unconscious knights strewn about the chamber, and tossing aside any of its minions that got in its way. A tall knight brandishing a bastard sword blocked its path. The demon threw back its head and laughed at the petty creature that opposed it. But its laugh was stifled when the cold steel of the warrior's holy blade sliced through its nigh impenetrable exoskeleton and punctured its innards. The beast howled in shock. Its golden eyes threatened to fly from their sockets; smoke and wisps of flame surged from its maw.

THE GATEWAY

Sir Gabriel Garn withdrew his war blade and slashed it back and forth across the demon's chest and shoulder, each time biting deeply into the living armor. Green blood surged from the jagged wounds as Korrgonn roared in anger and agony. Despite its grievous wounds, the creature raised its blade to parry Gabriel's next strike.

Gabriel slashed his blade in a mighty, sweeping arc, employing a fencing maneuver used only by the Picts of the Gray Waste, but Korrgonn countered it. Gabriel tried the spinning thrust maneuver taught him by the Emerald Elves, but Korrgonn effortlessly deflected it, already seeming to regain its strength. The infamous Dyvers thrusting maneuvers, the Dwarvish overhand strikes, the Cernian technique, the Sarnack maneuvers, and the Lengian cut and thrust style were all equally ineffective. Korrgonn countered them all. All the while, Gabriel dodged blow after titanic blow, and parried others with the flat of his blade. Although he countered Korrgonn's sword, the creature also made deft use of its spiked exoskeleton, slashing Gabriel several times, shredding his thick plate armor, and slicing into his flesh. Though Gabriel had perhaps never faced an opponent with such strength and resilience, he would not allow the fiend to defeat him. He had fought too many wars, too many duels over the ages to allow even one such as this to best him.

A spray of green blood and foul smelling ichor washed over Gabriel and a fiend's dismembered head hit his leg. A shout of "Doom!" came from nearby. The Lord Angle Theta was alive and had joined the fray!

Five fiends stalked Theta, who stood beside the corpse of one of their fellows, his silver-hued falchion dripping with ichor. When they met his steely gaze, the devils froze in their tracks and looks of terror formed on their grotesque visages.

"No!" bellowed one fiend, "It's the ancient enemy, the traitor!"

"We are betrayed, the humans knew of our coming," cried another. "Spare us Lord and we shall serve thee!" implored the fiend as it fell to its knees whimpering.

Theta's sword slashed by once, and then again, almost faster than the eye could follow, and both fiends' heads tumbled to the floor. The other three sprang toward him, overcoming whatever fear they felt. Working sword and shield to masterful perfection, Theta dodged, and parried, and cut, dealing out death and destruction as only he could. Moments later, he stood alone as his opponents' dismembered, twitching corpses littered the floor, green ichor pooling about his boots. As Theta moved to assist Gabriel, another thunderous roar emanated from the breach, this time much louder and deeper than before. More than a score of fiends scampered through the black hole, followed by a beast of incredible proportions. It struggled to expand the breach; its bulk far too large to fit through the six-foot wide portal.

Theta didn't even glance at his old friend Gabriel before turning to face this new threat. Theta charged toward the gateway and engaged the horde. He never looked back.

THE GATEWAY

Claradon stood alone against a trio of multi-armed fiends of wicked fangs and barbed tails. Three others of their ilk lay in a heap about the knight, having fallen victim to his desperate swordplay. He bashed one of his attackers back with his battered shield as he deflected and blocked blow after draining blow with his long sword. His strength was quickly ebbing; soon he'd have only his magic to sustain him.

He managed a series of furious counterstrikes that drove the devils back long enough for him to tap the sorcerous arts he'd honed as a Caradonian Knight. Through Odin's grace, he summoned a roaring column of flame from on high that engulfed one of the fiends, instantly incinerating it, its ashes crumbling to the stone floor. The remaining fiends turned and fled. Though calling down such power had drained him terribly, to Sir Gabriel's side he sprang, to aid him as best he could.

Claradon summoned all remaining mystical strength from deep within his very core and empowered one last sorcery. Unleashing his oldest and most forbidden words of arcane power, words he never dared utter before, he discharged a screeching blast of fiery death from the tip of his blade, a crackling azure bolt with the numinous energy to vaporize any man or beast. It struck Korrgonn unawares, enveloping its entire form in ravenous flame. But after only a moment, the flame's power waned, then vanished, consumed by the demon's stony soul. Claradon's magic was spent, though it mattered little since he commanded no words that could fell this abomination; that much was clear. But he had other tools.

His Dyvers blade in hand, he charged the beast. Though he struck with all his strength, his finely wrought steel blade merely bounced off Korrgonn's exoskeleton, sending sparks flying. Korrgonn ignored these ineffectual attacks and continued to parry Gabriel's deadly blows.

At last, Claradon's blade fractured against the thing's armor. Drawing his Asgardian dagger, he lunged in, thrusting the point at the fiend's back. To his surprise, the blade sliced through, puncturing its exoskeleton near where a man's kidney would be. Korrgonn howled in pain, spun around, and slammed the back of its spiked fist and forearm down on Claradon's head, crushing him to the floor where he lay bloodied and stunned.

Korrgonn maneuvered about and caught Gabriel's next blow with the hilt of its blade. It kicked Gabriel in the gut, sending him reeling backward, causing him to trip over and fall beyond Claradon. The beast stepped forward and raised its red blade high to finish Claradon who still lay dazed.

"No!" cried Gabriel. Bounding upward and forward over Claradon's prone form with blinding speed, Gabriel executed the reckless Valusian thrust maneuver taught him by Kull, king of that far-off land. Gabriel's war blade arced upward as he came in. The ensorcelled blade pierced Korrgonn's black heart, sending green ichor spurting everywhere. With all the knight's power behind the blow, the wide blade sunk halfway to the hilt. Completing the vicious maneuver,

Gabriel immediately pulled the sword back, nearly out the wound, before swiftly plunging it back in, sharply turning the blade as it entered. This merciless attack was designed to eviscerate the opponent, instantly sapping his strength, but it left much of the attacker's head and torso exposed. The chaos blade fell from the beast's grasp and its massive body dropped to its knees. It roared in pain and rage as its lifeblood showered the floor.

"I'll have your soul yet Gabriel," spat Korrgonn, as it threw an uppercut toward the knight's chest. Gabriel, in the midst of wrenching his sword free, moved to catch the blow in his gauntleted hand. But from Korrgonn's gnarled fist sprang a twelve-inch long barbed spike. It pierced clear through Gabriel's hand, and on through his thick steel breastplate, and sank deep into his chest. He stiffened at the blow and tried to pull away, only to have Korrgonn return the favor by twisting the blade and jabbing it in ever deeper.

The blow shocked Gabriel, but at first, he felt little pain. Dropping his sword, he pulled his Asgardian dagger from his belt and slashed it across Korrgonn's throat, once, twice, and a third time, slicing it from ear to ear. Blood and bile surged from both opponents' mouths. Still the beast held him fast.

Now the excruciating, indescribable pain washed over Gabriel, blasting him to his knees; Claradon's legs pinned beneath him.

From where he lay, only semi-conscious, Claradon attempted to let fly another magical blast, to come to his hero's aid, but his strength was spent. He couldn't even pull himself out from under Gabriel. He could do no more than watch in dazed horror as the ghastly scene unfolded before him. For him the battle was over.

Strangely, Korrgonn's arm began to glow a fiery red, first at the shoulder and soon extending down toward his fist. Gabriel continued to struggle to pull away, but the wicked spike would not release him. He felt it boring deep within his chest. It was moving, growing, twisting, probing. Probing for something. His heart? *Gods, how did it come to this? How to get away?*

The hellish glow permeating Korrgonn's body reached Gabriel, causing his chest to begin to glow as well. Coughing up blood, he tried in vain again to free himself. "No! No!" he gasped as he realized the fiend's mind. It was consuming his very body, devouring his immortal soul, assailing his mind, taking over his very being. He looked down and saw the blood draining from his chest. *This can't be happening, it can't be real. I cannot be defeated.*

Fleeting, ephemeral memories passed instantly before Gabriel's eyes and assailed his senses. A momentary image of smiting the fire wyrm of the Kronar Mountains; a mere wisp of the fetid stench of the barrow-wight who had killed those poor children. His duel with Valas Tearn, the assassin who had slain a thousand men; his conquest of the city of Saridden and of freeing its slaves; the great battle of Minoc-by-the-Sea; his victories over the demon-queen Krisona, and the vampire-lord Jaros, and the crazed master of the Dead Fens. A glimpse of that far off fateful day at R'lyeh when he and Theta banished the last of the fiends back from whence they came, back unto the void, and extracted some small measure of vengeance for the abominable plague that the beasts had unleashed upon mankind. That victory had freed all Midgaard from the yoke of chaos and bore witness to the dawning of a new age of freedom and hope. Gabriel would survive this battle, just as he had that day at R'lyeh. There could be no other outcome.

In desperation, he plunged his Asgardian dagger into Korrgonn's right eye, sinking it to the hilt. Still the spike held him fast.

His vision began to cloud; the sounds around him dimmed. He thought of the thousands of lives he'd saved down through the years, of all those he'd protected, of the uncountable mighty deeds he'd done.

He withdrew his dagger and plunged it into the beast's left eye. "Around me are my kinsmen, always," he said, and then pounded down on the hilt again, and again, and again.

He could see little now, and the sounds of the battle went away. He could hear his heart beating, the rushing of blood at his temples, but nothing else. *Can this be the end?* Everything moved in slow motion, the merest moments extending to long minutes. He thought of all the things important to him, all the places and the people he had known, all the lands he had visited, all that he would never do again.

"To the south, my father, my father's father, and all my line before them, back unto the beginning," he said, though only Claradon could hear him.

The evil glow covered nearly all his body, but Gabriel fought on and pounded down on the dagger's hilt again, and again, and again, and again.

"To the north is Odin…"

Visions of fire, floods, and terror flashed before his eyes.

He pounded down on the hilt again, and again, and again, and again, and again.

The world went dark, he could see no more.

The pain was less now.

"The hero's path."

Gabriel convulsed as the evil glow consumed him. He was alone. He would die alone.

Korrgonn's body stopped glowing and went limp.

Gabriel thought of the woman he'd loved and lost and forever longed for. If only he had another chance, if only he could do things over, if only he could be with her again…

His eyes closed and his head rolled to the side.

"The homeward road…"

He thought of his mother's face and her undying and unconditional love. If he could only see her one more time, if only he had more time…

"Valhalla".

Then he thought no more. And Sir Gabriel Garn passed into legend.

At last, Claradon's head began to clear and he dislodged himself from beneath Gabriel. Still dazed he flung himself into Korrgonn, ripping him away from Sir Gabriel. Claradon pounded his gauntleted fists into Korrgonn's unmoving head, Gabriel's dagger still protruding from its eye, over and over, mashing it to pieces. As he pummeled away, smoke rose from his hands and they began to burn. The acidic blood of the otherworldly beast actually ate through his gauntlets. He shed them before his flesh was sorely beset.

Claradon turned toward Gabriel, tears streaming down his face.

When Gabriel's eyes opened moments later, they glowed a brilliant gold. Claradon gasped in horror at the abominable sight, surmising exactly what it meant. He cried out for aid, but the din of the general melee drowned him out. Those terrible orbs were not Sir Gabriel's eyes at all; they were the eyes of the Son of Azathoth, the Prince of Demons. Claradon couldn't believe his eyes – so stunned was he that he couldn't move.

Gabriel's mouth opened and it spewed out a gory glob of blood. The wound on his chest glowed for a moment and then rapidly closed and healed itself. It grinned an evil, unholy grin, picked up Korrgonn's sword as it stood up, turned, and fled the building.

XIII
YOUR TIME HAS COME AND GONE

The enormous monstrosity at the breach broke its way through and entered Midgaard. As it did so, its form shrunk and transformed into the likeness of a huge, handsome, armored knight wielding a mammoth, crimson sword. No one could mistake its dark, unholy visage. This beast was none other than Bhaal, the infamous lord of death and chaos. It paused at the hell-mouth for several moments surveying the carnage taking place in its ancient temple. It laughed. Not a laugh of mirth; not the laugh of a man. It was a maniacal, inhuman cackling, such as had not been inflicted on the ears of man for untold epochs. The beast was here now, on our world. It would make it his again. It had won.

As a multitude of smaller fiends leaped through the gateway and moved to engage Lord Theta - Dolan and Sirs Artol, Glimron, Talbot, and Dalken closed with the transformed fiend from its flanks. With blinding speed, Bhaal struck a brutal overhand blow at the largest of the warriors, Artol, who swiftly raised his battle-axe to parry the blow, but the massive strike sheared the axe haft cleanly in half. Bhaal's red sword rotated with the impact and the flat of the blade struck Artol squarely atop his helm. His eyes rolled back in his head as he crumpled to the floor.

Dolan lunged in and stabbed Bhaal in the sternum, burying his glowing dagger in the fiend's chest. Bhaal roared, grabbed Dolan by the throat, and lifted him high. As Talbot moved in, Bhaal threw Dolan into him, sending them both cascading across the ebony slab.

Glimron and Dalken simultaneously struck at Bhaal's legs. Their steel blades clanged loudly and sparked when they struck the chaos-wrought armor, but had no damaging effect. Bhaal's next cut entered Glimron's right shoulder, cleaving clean through him, coming out his left side. Bhaal grabbed Dalken by the throat and lifted him up. The fiend opened its mouth, wide like a serpent, and a two-pronged, pincer-like object flew out and plunged into Dalken's eyes. The

THE GATEWAY

pincers retracted, and ripped the knight's eyes from their sockets.

Bhaal held Dalken aloft for several seconds as he screamed in agony before it tightened its grip and crushed the knight's throat. It flung the corpse away as if it weighed nary a pound.

Nearby, Lord Theta's whirling blade sliced off fiendish arms and legs with abandon. No fiend could stand against him for more than moments. Even the press of numbers could not turn the tide against him. The corpses of the demons piled high about him in gruesome heaps. He was an unstoppable juggernaut. He was death incarnate. The last thing each of his foes heard was his booming mantra, "Doom! Doom!" He finished off the last of them and stepped over the pile of corpses to engage Bhaal.

"You've slain my minions, mortal," said Bhaal, his voice now a rich baritone, to the bloody knight that stood before him. "Impressive. But you cannot stand against a Lord of Chaos!"

Theta sheathed his blade and picked up his lance which still lay at the base of the altar and brandished it as a spear.

"Do you not know me, creature? Has it been so long?"

Lord Bhaal's mouth dropped open. "You?! You will not thwart us again, harbinger of doom. Not again! We will have this world back, traitor. We shall cleanse it by fire and sword and you'll not stop us. What once was ours will be ours again."

"This be no place for you Bhaal," shouted Theta. "You don't belong here. Your time has come and gone;

it be our time now." Theta stalked cautiously toward the beast, looking for an opening to use his lance. "I shall put you down as I have your brethren. You'll sleep with them in the void."

As Bhaal began to advance, it was struck by a large glowing, floating mace that appeared from nowhere. The mace pummeled Bhaal about the head and chest forcing it backward. Bhaal swung its sword wildly, but there was no foe for it to smite. The sword passed through the spectral mace and could do it no harm. One wild swing caught the edge of the stone altar, shearing off a large chunk while barely slowing the mammoth blade.

Theta, mouthing ancient words of power, pointed the tip of his lance at Bhaal and a sparkling arc of electricity rocketed from it and crashed into the beast's chest. Its breastplate blackened, charred, and fell off, exposing the reddish leather-like flesh beneath. The beast roared in pain but continued to swing its sword frantically, slicing nothing but air.

Par Tanch's magical orbs blasted into Bhaal. One struck its exposed chest, tearing into the beast and causing some damage; the others bounced harmlessly off Bhaal's chaos-wrought armor. The enchanted mace, also controlled by Par Tanch's arcane arts, continued to pummel Bhaal and caused him to stagger farther backward, toward the breach.

Dolan skulked his way on hands and knees behind Bhaal who was oblivious to his presence. Dolan saw Theta moving in with his lance and carefully positioned himself just in front of the breach, and directly behind Bhaal. Distracted by the array of magical attacks assailing it, Bhaal could not react in time to counter Theta's lance. Theta lunged forward and buried its sharpened tip deep into the breast of the chaos lord. A look of shock and agony formed on Bhaal's face as the lance sunk in and thrust him backward.

"Give my regards to Arioch," shouted Theta. "Tell him I have not forgotten, and I will yet have my revenge."

Bhaal roared in anger, as he struggled against Theta, who used the lance to push him inexorably backward.

"Curse you, traitor," spat Bhaal. "You'll pay for this threefold - three evils to you I promise. So do I curse thee."

As Theta pushed the beast back, it tripped over Dolan, just as Dolan had planned. It fell backward over him and tumbled right through the gateway, back whence it came. Bhaal fell out of sight, into the utter blackness beyond, roaring more curses at Theta as it fell; Theta's lance still buried in its chest.

XIV
THE LORD OF THE LAND

Soon only the moans and wails of the wounded filled the air.

"We killed them all boss," said Dolan. "All except the skull-faced one, what came out first. But we lost a lot of the shiny men."

"It's not over yet, Dolan. We must close the gateway or countless more fiends will soon come through. If that happens, all Midgaard will be lost."

"Let them come," said Artol, as he pulled himself to his feet beside the altar. A thin stream of blood trickling down the side of his head. "We can take them."

Ignoring the overconfident sergeant, Theta began searching the floor around the altar. "Find the shards of the black orb, they must be holding the gateway open."

More roars, howls and maddening gibbering began anew from somewhere beyond the breach, although no new fiends could yet be seen.

"Another wave comes," Theta shouted over the increasing din. "I'll hold fast the portal. You must destroy the shards. But don't touch them with your flesh or you'll surely die."

"Here it is," shouted Dolan, as he pointed to a glowing piece of obsidian on the floor.

Claradon stepped up next to Dolan holding a large hammer. "For my father!" he shouted as he slammed the hammer down onto the shard, smashing it to tiny pieces. The gateway instantly disappeared and the chaotic din abruptly stopped. Where the gateway once was, now remained only the crumbled back wall of the sinister temple.

Before the men could rejoice in their victory, a loud rumbling began. Within moments, the very earth beneath their feet began to shake. They heard roaring and rumbling sounds like those produced by a herd of

THE GATEWAY

large beasts. Mammoth chunks of stone fell from the high ceiling.

"The whole place is collapsing," said Dolan.

"Grab the wounded and get them out of here," shouted Theta.

They did so and fled as the otherworldly structure collapsed around them. Two minutes after the earth began to shake; the evil edifice was no more. Only a mound of rubble and a cloud of dust remained. Those that made it out of the temple lay strewn about the circle of desolation. Some collapsed from exhaustion; some collapsed from blood loss; still others were already dead. Strangely, the sun was beginning to rise. It was dawn. Somehow, the bizarre atmosphere within the temple's depths had distorted the flow of time itself, turning what seemed like no more than minutes into more than six hours.

Young Sir Paldor was immediately sent ahead to Dor Eotrus to summon aid, stopping only for a few minutes to bandage the wound on his chest. Tanch and Claradon set about to aid the wounded in the party. Theta and Dolan searched for sign of the skull-faced fiend that had fled the temple. They found no trail, no spoor of the beast. It had vanished. They found the corpses of six knights at the edge of the circle. Apparently, they had fled during the battle and were killed by the skull-faced fiend or some other horror that had also escaped.

After a short while, the survivors gathered about and Sir Glimador reported the casualty list. Eighteen knights were confirmed dead, eleven others were missing and presumed buried in the collapsed temple.

Of Dor Eotrus's soldiers only Glimador, Artol, Indigo, Paldor, and Claradon still lived.

To everyone's astonishment, Sir Gabriel was amongst the missing. Nearly all the survivors were wounded to varying degrees, although most not seriously.

Theta was a bloody mess, covered in ichor and gore from head to toe, though little, if any of the blood seemed to be his.

Once the men had caught their breath, Claradon recounted what he saw of the epic battle between Korrgonn and Sir Gabriel - even Theta listened intently. All were shocked at Gabriel's gruesome fate. "The skalds will tell of that battle for ages to come," said Artol, tears streaming down his face.

"Perhaps Sir Gabriel still lives," Claradon said, as he saw to Ob's grievous wound, only half believing there was some hope. "Perhaps we can free him of the influence of the monster."

"I just cannot believe this," said Ob, "Aradon gone, and Brother Donnelin, Talbon, Stern, and now Gabriel. How could this happen? Nobody could beat Gabriel. Nobody." His hand reached for his wineskin, but it was lost.

"It's the end of the world," said Tanch. "I told you it was coming – no one wanted to listen, but I foretold it. These are the end times."

Overcome by all that had happened, Claradon dropped to both knees and wept. His father and his mentor both destroyed at the hands of chaos, and so many other friends and comrades as well. It was all

THE GATEWAY

too much; his head was swimming. He gripped Ob's shoulder, closed his eyes, and recited a prayer to Odin.

"Steady boy," said Ob, his voice weak from his wounds and his eyes only half opened, "You're the Lord of the Land now. You mustn't show weakness in front of the troops." Due to his wounds, Ob apparently didn't realize that nearly all 'the troops' were dead.

"Perhaps, we can cast out the monster from Sir Gabriel. We must find him," said Tanch.

"I'm doubting it pal," said Ob weakly, "Gabe's the toughest warrior this side of Odin. Ain't nothing, not even some stinking chaos lord as can take him over if he's alive. He's dead and it took his corpse I say. And that's the end of him."

"Oh my. Don't say such things Master Ob; we have to try the save him."

"The gnome speaks truly," said Theta. "Gabriel is lost. There's nothing we can do for him save to avenge him."

Theta pulled a metallic flask from his belt; uncorked the top and put it to Ob's lips. "You fought bravely, gnome," said Theta. "Drink this; it will strengthen you." Ob did so. Almost at once the flow of blood from Ob's wound stopped and color returned to his face.

The survivors soon headed back to the Dor as fast as they dared. With them they brought as many of their fallen comrades as they could manage, including Lord Eotrus's body, what little remained of it. Patrols would soon return for the rest of the honored dead.

On the way, Par Tanch approached Claradon. He spoke in a stronger, deeper, and steadier voice than was his custom. "Brother Claradon," he said, taking care that no one else overheard, "Though I know this timing is poor, I must advise you that the Order of the Arcane, and likely the Crown, for reasons of their own, will never allow the events of last night to be known. They will cover it up. Some story will be fabricated to account for the battle, the howling in the woods, the fog. They will force you and your officers to swear to never reveal the truth."

Claradon's eyes narrowed as he was taken aback by these words. "And what if I don't go along with these lies? What if I want everyone to know the truth of how father and Sir Gabriel died?"

"Then they will destroy you. You'll lose the Dor and your good name, perhaps even your very life."

"Would they really go so far? Could they?"

"They would, they could, and they've done such things before. I've seen it."

"But King Tenzivel has always been a friend to us. He would never allow this."

"The king is old, Claradon. Dark voices whisper in his ear these days. Things are changing in Lomion, my friend, and not for the better - we cannot count on the King's support."

"Then what are we to do?"

"Let us be the ones to create the tale. That way we can be assured that Lord Eotrus, Sir Gabriel, and the others are honored as the heroes that they are. We can say that a pack of trolls came down from the mountains and caused all the trouble. There was a time when trolls rampaged through these lands, causing much death and destruction. Though rarely seen these days, they're still much feared and are considered extremely deadly. Any knight that fell in battle to a pack of such beasts whilst protecting his lands would be rightly named a hero."

"And how would we explain the wailing in the night?"

"We'd say it was the trolls. Few alive in these parts have ever heard the call of a troll. If we say that that's what they heard, most would believe us."

"And the fog and the thundering explosions the night father was lost?"

"A freakish storm, nothing more. Claradon, I know this is difficult, but we must do this. We must protect the Eotrus name or your enemies will use this opportunity to destroy you. We've little choice in this. Besides, we'll always know the truth. The people will know that our comrades died as heroes defending the Dor. What does it matter that people think they fell to trolls rather than chaos demons? A hero is a hero."

"Very well, very well. For the sake of my brothers, I'll go along with this. But know well, if it were only my position and my life at stake, I'd tell the Order to go to hell, and the Crown too, if need be."

"I don't doubt it, Master Claradon."

"What of Paldor? He's likely telling the tale even now."

"He hit his head in the battle. He became delusional and wandered off. He didn't know what he was saying."

"You think of everything, don't you, Par Tanch."

"It's my job, Sir. It's my job. We'll not be able to keep the truth from the senior knights at the Dor though. You'll have to swear them to secrecy and all of us here as well, of course."

"It will be done."

Claradon awoke in his bed to Ob shaking him. "Get off your duff you lazy bugger! The men are in the great hall already. We need to get you down there right quick. Mr. Know-it-All, fancy pants, is giving a speech. The boys need to know you're the boss now, not that foreigner, nor anybody else."

Claradon's head still spun from the tale Ob told him the previous night, as Claradon stood by the wounded gnome's bedside. The last days seemed a maddened dream. Claradon pulled himself together as best he could, splashing some water on his face to revive himself. He strapped on his sword belt and headed to the great hall.

In the interests of keeping their secret, knights guarded the doors, only admitting ranking knights who knew the truth of what happened in the wood. When Ob and Claradon arrived, Theta was standing at the forefront, addressing the men. The knights were rallying around him, bristling for a fight, enraged as they were over the loss of their Lord and their comrades. Each time Theta spoke, the knights quieted down.

"We have to destroy his body," Theta boomed in his strong, steady voice. "When we do, we'll be killing Korrgonn, not Gabriel. But it won't be easy. Korrgonn not only has all of his own knowledge and skills, but now he also has Gabriel's. Now he's far more dangerous than ever before. Now he knows all that Gabriel knew. No one will be safe until we put him down. And do not forget the skull-faced demon – that creature was Mortach of Chaos. He must be destroyed as well."

"Oh my," said Tanch. "Two Chaos Lords running about; it's the end."

Artol stepped forward. "We must find them and destroy them for what they've done, however difficult the task."

"We shall track our enemies to the ends of Midgaard, and beyond if need be," boomed Theta. "We shall cleanse the world of their plague."

A cheer erupted in the hall, the knights rose to their feet and shook their fists.

"There can be no other course of action," boomed Theta.

After the noise died down, Tanch said, "This sounds like we're embarking on a major undertaking. It may be that my delicate back isn't up to the challenge. Perhaps I can do more good tending to the wounded or praying to Odin in support of this valiant quest."

The knights laughed at the cowardly wizard and poked fun at him.

Claradon moved through the ranks. "No, Par Tanch. I'll need you in this. You'll come with us. We shall go back to the Vermion, to the circle and pick up the trail of the chaos lords. We'll not return until we rid this world of them."

Ob cleared the way ahead of Claradon. "All right, Theta, move aside," shouted Ob, pushing through the troops to the front of the hall. Theta glared at the gnome, stood his ground, but said nothing.

"Claradon is here now and will be taking over." Ob climbed atop a table and turned to the gathered knights, his arms upraised. He motioned for quiet. "Brother Claradon, as first son of House Eotrus, and upon Lord Aradon's passing, is now Lord of the Dor, and Patriarch of House Eotrus. You will serve him with the same respect and honor with which you served Aradon afore him. And if you don't, I'll rip your stinking heads off!"

"Long live Lord Claradon," boomed Artol, from amidst the knights.

"Long live Lord Claradon," shouted all the knights in response.

"And death to the Chaos Lords," boomed Artol, standing and raising his fist to the air.

"Death to the Chaos Lords," boomed the whole company in retort.

"I guess we won't be going home anytime soon, Lord Angle," whispered Dolan.

"Not for some time, Dolan."

"When do you think them evil-doers will leave us be so we can live like regular folks?"

"When I've killed them all; not before."

XV
EPILOGUE

Many years later.

The appointed hour is at hand. Our wait will soon be over. I still cannot believe this - my most feared nightmare has come to pass. I've dreaded this day for so long; I've prayed it would never come. But it's here - it's now. There were so many things I wanted to do before this fateful day. If only I had more time.

But there is no more time for memories, no more visiting with the shades of my past-- now is the time for action, for courage, and for sacrifice. This time - I lead. I am the rock that must steady the troops. I wield the sword that will carry the day - or condemn us to everlasting defeat. This is my burden. I carry it alone.

I can hear my men stirring in the camp outside. The clinking and clanking of many armored men, the sounds of a hundred swords being pulled from their scabbards. I'm ready. I will make my father proud.

A great wind came up, and the air suddenly grew unnaturally chill. Brother Claradon Eotrus, Lord of Dor Eotrus, rose, adjusted his sword belt. and picked up his shield. Moments later, his Knight Captain and his House Wizard rushed into the command tent; fearful looks etched their faces.

"Lord Eotrus," said the wizard, "It's time. The fog has returned!"

END

GLOSSARY

PLACES

The Realms
Asgard: legendary home of the gods
Lomion: a great kingdom of Midgaard
Midgaard: the world of man
Nifleheim: the realm of the Chaos Lords
Vaeden: paradise, lost

Places Within The Kingdom Of Lomion
Dor Eotrus: fortress and lands ruled by House Eotrus, north of Lomion City
Dor Lomion: fortress within Lomion City, ruled by House Harringgold
Dor Malvegil: fortress and lands ruled by House Malvegil, southeast of Lomion City on the west bank of the Grand Hudsar River
Dyvers: Lomerian city known for its quality metalworking
Lomion City (aka Lomion): capitol city of the Kingdom of Lomion
Riker's Crossroads: Village at the southern border of Eotrus lands
Tammanian Hall: high seat of government in Lomion; home of the High Council and the Council of Lords
Tower of the Arcane: high seat of wizardom; in Lomion City
Vermion Forest: foreboding wood west of Dor Eotrus

PEOPLE

House Eotrus
The Eotrus rule the fortress of Dor Eotrus, the Outer Dor (a town outside the fortress walls) and the surrounding lands for many leagues.

Aradon Eotrus, Lord: (pronounced Eee-oh-tro`-sss) – Patriarch of the House (presumed dead)
Claradon Eotrus, Brother: (Clara-don) Eldest son of Aradon, Caradonian Knight
Ector Eotrus, Sir: Third son of Aradon
Gabriel Garn, Sir: House Weapons Master
Jude Eotrus, Sir: Second son of Aradon
Knights & Soldiers of the House: Artol 'The Destroyer', Sir Paldor, Sir Glimador Malvegil, Sir Indigo,
Malcolm Eotrus: Fourth son of Aradon
Ob A. Faz III: (Ahb A. Fahzz) Castellan and Master Scout of Dor Eotrus, a gnome
Tanch Trinagal, Par: (Trin-ah-ghaal) of the Blue Tower; Son of Sinch; House Wizard for the Eotrus

House Harringgold
Harper Harringgold, Lord: Arch-Duke of Lomion City; Patriarch of the House; Lord of Dor Lomion
Grim Fischer: agent of Harper, a gnome

The Lords of Chaos
Azathoth: god worshipped by the Chaos Lords and The Shadow League
Arioch; Bhaal; Hecate; Mortach
Korrgonn, Lord Gallis: son of Azathoth

Others Of Note

Angle Theta, Lord: (Thay`-tah) (aka Thetan) knight errant and nobleman from a far-off land beyond the sea.
Caradonian Knights: priestly order of knights
Dolan Silk: (Doe`-lin) Theta's manservant
Myrdonians: Royal Lomerian Knights
Pipkorn: (aka Rascatlan) former Grand Master of the Tower of the Arcane. A wizard.
Volsungs: men/humans

THINGS

Miscellany

Asgardian Daggers: legendary weapons created in the first age of Midgaard. They can harm creatures of Nifleheim.
    Dargus Dal: Gabriel's Asgardian dagger
    Worfin Dal: "Lord's Dagger," Claradon's Asgardian dagger
Dor: a fortress
Dyvers Blades: finely crafted steel swords

ABOUT THE AUTHOR

For over twenty years, Glenn G. Thater has written works of fiction and historical fiction focusing on the genres of heroic fantasy and sword and sorcery. His published works include the first three volumes of the Harbinger of Doom saga - *The Gateway, The Fallen Angle,* and *Knight Eternal,* and the short story *The Hero and the Fiend* which appears in the anthology *Shameless Shorts.*

Mr. Thater holds degrees in Physics and Engineering, and is a practicing licensed professional engineer specializing in forensic investigations of building failures and other disasters. He's an author of numerous scientific papers, magazine articles, technical reports, and engineering textbook chapters. He's presented papers at engineering congresses throughout the United States and internationally on such topics as the World Trade Center collapses, bridge collapses, and on the construction and analysis of the United States Capital Dome in Washington D.C.

Many of Mr. Thater's stories (and story excerpts) are posted on his official website http://www.angletheta.blogspot.com, where fans may leave comments and questions.

Printed in Great Britain
by Amazon